Mark of the Tattoo

By Cheryl Castro

ewpublishing.com

Published by
Eagle's Wings Publishing
Central Point, OR 97502

2008 ©Cheryl Castro

Cover Illustration By Emily Burdge

ISBN -10:   0-9819362-2-9
ISBN -13:   978-0-9819362-2-2

Mark of the Tattoo

By Cheryl Castro

ACKNOWLEDGMENTS

When a person tackles an important project, like writing a novel, they need to have a support group. Otherwise, to be successful is almost impossible.

I would like to thank those who so diligently supported me. They have my love and gratitude:

Suzy Leggett and Winnie Nichols, my two best friends who gave me encouragement-

Margaret Bradburn, who helped with editing and continuing ideas for public exposure –

Sandy Cathcart, my writing instructor who showed me the basic skills

Finally my patient and loving husband R.C. who continually read, reread and reread … ad infinitum.

Table of Contents

Prologue

Descriptions, Facts, and Information

This is a story about a fourteen-year-old boy named Uri. He is living among the Pinola Tribe on the planet, Terrasa. The tribes in the story, the Pinola and the Dombara, occupy two continents separated by the Green Sea. A vast, shallow ocean that encompasses Terrasa. Because of this, waves are small even during wild storms, and little or no beach erosion ever happens.

This is a planet similar to our Earth with similar seasons, however the years and length of days are slightly shorter. The sun is a medium size, one hundred and three million miles away so the planet's temperature is a bit cooler. There are two moons, the larger one is Venca, (the first), and the other is a bit smaller Visca, (the second). They rise and set at different intervals from each other. The orbits are such that they are both full at the same time every two hundred years.

The inhabitants are human. They all are one race. However, the areas they live in have influenced some of their characteristics. Their eyes are either orange, brown, or ice blue. The hair color ranges from light blonde to golden brown. The adults are 5'6" to 5'10". Their bone structure is similar. Their cheek bones are high and their eyes, almond shaped.

But their eyelids have a fold like our Caucasian race. They have a high immune system and are very healthy, no cold or flu virus. Mentally and emotionally they are just like us.

Their development is still primitive. They live in tribal villages, with no mechanization. Some tribes make clothing, some furniture, and other items. All tribes are agrarian, but grain grows only in the Dombara Land. They all get along fairly well except for one, the Bast Tribe, but they all trade with each other within their respective lands. The language is the same for all tribes. The Bast have a pidgin-type dialect, also there is an ancient language, and many things are named from that.

The northern continent is Piucha, an arid land that consists of dunes and areas of rock with sand. The north-west area, near the sea, is rocky and has a small, low mountain range. The climate is warm with a hot season of a few weeks. The Pinola Tribe live in the south by the sand dunes. The Pinola's diet is mainly vegetarian. They don't eat the animals they raise for milk. They live in earthen huts with thatched roofs from palm-like branches.

There is scant rainfall, but many ancient wells exist throughout the land, and maintained by the nearby tribes, but shared by all. The Pinolas have created irrigation canals from some of them. The wells tend to get low often and all the tribes on this land need a better diet. There is a small desert worm, the wona. It grows to three or four feet long. A delicacy that is hard to hunt down, but a necessary part of their meager, protein deficient diet.

To their east are the Brown Hills separated by a valley where there are many caves. All are off limits to everyone because of the belief they are homes to the Evil Spirits that rule the land.

South from there the land enters the area of the seashore and there is a small, sandy beach. The sea is only accessible here and at the cone-shaped isthmus to the southwest. As the land goes east, it rises and northeast of the Brown Hills are cliffs made of sandstone that drop to the sea. On the east side of the isthmus in the south-west, there also are cliffs overlooking the sea.

To the north live the Yoka Tribe. Their land is sand and rocks. They also live mainly on vegetables along with insects. They are a bit more advanced, and tend to possess more curiosity about the world. Therefore, they instituted a learning system, and share a school with the Pinola Tribe.

To the southwest are the Rabir. These people are darker skinned, living where the sun is stronger and hotter. Their land is all sand and they are nomads, living in tents, herding goat and sheep-like animals. Even the Pinolas raise goat-like animals. They are called Kavacs, a single one a Kavac. The sheep are Bamea. They raise them mainly for milk, skins, and wool. Much too valuable to kill and eat. There are no snakes on Piucha, but many lizard and insects inhabit the land and the Yoka eat those.

All the tribes have a governing system that consists of a council of elders picked by the existing chief at the time a replacement is required. The chief is replaced only by death, but the rest have a time limit to their office. The tribes on this land all believe in evil spirits and curses. Much superstition and fear abounds.

The land far to the north has not been explored, because of the fear of evil spirits. A road comes down from the area and is blocked by many talisman, each tribe's specific charm for their specific superstitions. It winds east to the Yoka territory then sharply west and down through the west side of the Pinola land. It continues east again into the valley by the caves and to the sea. A rudimentary road enters the Rabir land by the Pinola well, but ends out in the desert. Far to the west, by the sea, there are rumors that underwater sea caves exist. No one yet, has had the nerve to explore them.

***

Across the Green Sea to the south lies the larger continent of Dombara. This land is much different. Lush and green because there is much rainfall. There are forests and grasslands throughout the land. The weather systems come across the northwest, and pick up moisture from the Green Sea, dropping rain as it reaches land. Many rivers run from the hills down to the sea. The north end of the continent is in a temperate zone. The temperature is mild and even. Further south there is a rumor that ice and snow exist in the winter.

The Dombara tribe lives at the north-west tip of the land. They are the largest and the most ancient tribe in the two lands, and there is evidence all other tribes descended from them. Their society raises poultry, dairy animals, and many crops. They have a well-organized education system and they have perfected the art of sailing and fishing. Much of their diet comes from the sea. The boats range from 14 to 20 feet. Their market place is extensive and all the tribes in the Dombara land buy and sell there. Still, there is no mechanization. The people are satisfied and well fed. Their main buildings are constructed of a silvery stone mined from an ancient area. They have books made of thin papyrus-type paper.

They share the land with other tribes. The Mudan, the Bast, and the Mountain People. The Mudan people live east of the Dombara village, by the Mudan River. The road to get there begins at the edge of the Dombara village, crosses the Dombara River with a footbridge, forks with one heading east, crossing the Pic River through the forest and into the village. The main road continues south, forks again further south. The Mudan have their own school, but depend on the Dombaras for schoolbooks and materials. They also employ the Dombara priests for their religious activities.

The elusive Mountain People are scattered south-west through the forest past the Sho and Shai Rivers, between the Tol and Nui Rivers. The main road, after the second fork, narrows and follows the Sho River. The large Nui River originates in the high hills, continues winding to the south, and empties into Jocoo Bay. Here there are beaches scattered at the south end of the rivers where they empty into the sea.

South of the Dombara Village are forests. The Bast River also begins high in the hills, but in the east, and runs directly south. The Bast live southeast, near the coast. A primitive road cuts east from the second fork of the main road. It travels through a heavy forested area to the Bast River. Because there is no bridge on this river, it is dangerous to cross. The Bast people like it that way because they are not a friendly tribe. They are secretive and treacherous. It is said they have a secret way to cross the river. Some stories even say they become spirits and fly across.

North of their village near the Bast River, is where the medicinal trees grow. The Bast bring bark and powder they make from the trees and roots to the Dombara market place to sell as medicine. They make beautiful furniture crafted from the Tangleroot Tree. These are highly coveted. People put in orders for products. Then those products have a tendency to increase in price much too often. The Bast also sell their special seasonal fruits. These are a real treat because those fruit trees grow nowhere else on the land.

The other tribes have tried to negotiate for better communication with the Bast, but haven't succeeded in changing the attitude of this tribe who jealously guard their treasures. They do not allow visitors in their land. It is heavily forested, cooler, and wetter than the north area. In addition, very dangerous. The Bast people have a long coastal area and guard it with high lookouts made of wood from the trees in their area. They also have many weapons, spears, and bows with arrows that they tip with various poisons. The other tribes only have knives and small spears for hunting and fishing. The other tribes do not know how far south the Basts have extended their territory, but there are rumors of an extension village in the grassy plains to the south, near the ice floes. There is much mystery about these difficult people.

While the Pinolas and the tribes that live around them believe evil spirits dominate the land, the Mudans and the Dombaras believe in one God with three personalities, a triune deity, The Creator of All, His son the Savior, and His Spirit. Many men make up a priesthood that keep the ancient Books, leading the people in worship of the Creator and the Savior. The Bast have many gods and are pantheistic.

Chapter One

Pinola Land

The sand dunes shimmered under the crystalline, blue sky. Like an unyielding tide, they covered most of the land where the Pinola Tribe lived.

In the southern dune area, not far from the village, Uri lay very still, his body flattened on the sand as he attempted to erase any shadows. Even though the hot Terrassan sun hammered down on his brown skin, he was oblivious to everything but what lay directly in front of him. Spending most of his time on the dunes, he knew them better than anyone did.

The sun was overhead as Uri patiently waited for his prey. If the wona didn't appear soon, the heat would drive it deeper into the sand. It had to be now, or he would have to try again, another day. The very thought of the fat, four-foot-long worm, roasting over the cooking fire made his mouth water. He could almost taste the delicate, sweet meat that lay under the hard scales.

A good hunter would know which direction the wona headed as it lifted from the sand by determining the pattern of the scales. A good hunter would know how and when to throw the deadly grag, a long, slender wooden pole with a sharp metal s-shaped hook.

Uri wanted more than to be a good hunter. He wanted to be known as a great hunter.

He watched, focused, for any movement beneath the sand. In his right fist, he held the grag. It hung, in the air, over his shoulder as he waited, anticipating. He blended into the landscape, quiet and still like the air.

Grains of sand began to tremble, and in a flash, the wona was there. Uri was ready as the worm lifted its body into the air. The grag rammed into the sand, buried deep, but was still and barren. Disgusted, Uri stood and glared at the weapon in the sand. He had bungled the one chance to catch his prey at this location. He leaned over to retrieve the grag. He could try again in the small dunes north of the village, but the worms weren't as large in that area. The best hunting grounds were at the edge of the great, high dunes where the land dipped sharply to the far basin.

His feet, covered only with the traditional brown cloth foot bindings, wrapped from the toes to the ankles, had plowed under the sand as he stood still, holding the weapon.

He gazed past the rolling dunes down to the wide, desolate valley at the foot of the Brown Hills. In all his fourteen years, he had never seen a living thing down at the edge of those hills, but today he spotted a small patrol of Dombaras, the tribe from across the Green Sea. He knew they were Dombara from the colorful clothing. They always decorated their vests with rows of beading, and they wore their hair pulled back in one long braid. Their voices echoed across the valley, but the words were not clear.

Uri's heart began to pound. He crouched and watched the men disappear into a cave below. That cave, forbidden to all the Pinola children such as Uri, must be a terrible place. Even the grownups stayed away from that area, because the evil spirits that roamed the valley made their home in all those caves. An electrified shiver of fear flashed through Uri's body. What could these people want here in his land, in these caves? Why were they here?

As he concentrated on the scene unfolding in the valley below, he sensed a movement behind him. Whirling, he suddenly found himself staring into the eyes of a small boy dressed in Dombara clothing. He was surprised at the boy's orange eyes. Only the children of Uri's tribe had that color eyes. Therefore, he was surprised to see children of other tribes did also. Uri lifted his grag.

"Hello." The boy greeted him, smiling. "I'm Bibbi, who are you?"

Grimly, Uri stared into those eyes, but all he saw was a guileless, innocent smile. "My name is Uri." He answered gruffly, continuing a defensive posture.

"You're a Pinola, aren't you?" Bibbi continued. "I'm a Dombara. I'm not supposed to be up here, but I wanted to see what this land looked like. We don't have any sand dunes in my home." He looked at the weapon. "What's that?

"A grag." Uri said, looking into the valley below. Suspicion of this boy's appearance played in his mind. How did he find his way up here? Were more on their way?

"What were you doing?" Bibbi asked.

"I am a hunter." Uri proudly pointed to his pole. "I'm hunting the wona."

Bibbi frowned. "What's a wona?"

"Meat." Uri said, puffing out his chest. Meat was an important food for the Pinolas, and being a hunter of meat was an important job. "I'm a hunter of meat."

"I saw you miss." Bibbi said.

Choosing to ignore the comment Uri asked, "Why are your people here in my land?"

Bibbi plopped to the ground and picked up a handful of sand, sifting it through his fingers. Uri crouched next to him, waiting for an answer.

9

"We came over in big boats." Bibbi answered, looking up at the hot sun. "Our fathers bring their sons with them on voyages. It's our way."

"I find that strange. Why did they go into those caves? They are full of evil spirits." Uri motioned, again looking into the valley now empty "Do your people worship them?"

"Oh no. We worship the One who created the Universe." Bibbi looked up at Uri. "We aren't afraid of evil spirits. They have no power over us."

Uri was skeptical. "Have you been in those caves yourself?"

"We camped in them, and I haven't seen spirits of any kind." Bibbi said, with a taunting edge to his voice.

Uri was amazed. What kind of power did these people have? "How long do your people plan to stay?"

"I think we are leaving in a few days. At least that's what I heard."

Uri watched Bibbi play with the sand.

"We don't have sand where I live." Bibbi said, "We have grass and trees, and dirt."

That ignited Uri's curiosity. "What is dirt?"

"It's like sand, only heavier and gritty. It's brown."

"Oh, we have sandy dirt." Uri smiled. "It's where we grow our crops."

"We grow crops too." Bibbi was not to be outdone. "We grow grass for our animals to eat. Then they give us milk."

"We have animals that give us milk. They are small with white hair and have little horns." Uri wiggled his fingers on either side of his head.

"Our animals are big and taller than me," Bibbi puffed out his chest, "and they give buckets of milk."

Uri could tell this was growing into a contest. "You don't have the wona," he said proudly.

Bibbi frowned. "No. We don't have wonas."

Uri enjoyed talking to the boy, and he made Uri smile, something he seldom did. "You have strange things in your land." He shook his head. "Our tribe has never visited your land. I would like to come sometime and see those things for myself."

Bibbi jumped to his feet. "Please come and visit me. I would like that."

Uri stood and put his hands on Bibbi's shoulders. "Let's meet here tomorrow at the same time."

"I'll be here," promised Bibbi. He turned disappearing down the back of the dunes from where he came.

Again, Uri turned to watch the mouth of the caves where the Dombara men had entered. He wasn't sure what to make of the whole thing. Did they associate with the Evil Spirits? On the other hand, as Bibbi said, nothing was there. Uri enjoyed the friendship that was building between Bibbi and himself. The Dombaras didn't seem to be making any problems. Besides what trouble could they cause? They had their families with them. Uri started for home, empty-handed without dinner. He decided for now, he would keep the event to himself, and he looked forward to seeing Bibbi the next day.

Chapter Two
A Successful Hunt

Uri enjoyed the last two days they had spent together. Bibbi had wanted to learn to throw the grag so Uri carefully instructed him.

"You must be able to hold it over your head for a long time, and be poised, ready. If you move just before you throw it, the wona will sense your presence and bury deeper in the sand."

Then a lizard scampered across the hot sand. Bibbi jumped and threw the grag, but the lizard saw him, and moved in the opposite direction.

"See," Uri scolded. "I told you, these creatures have a built-in instinct. You have to be motionless and quick. It has to happen in less than a heartbeat."

Today Uri had been successful in the hunt, and best of all, his new friend Bibbi had been there to watch him. They lay hidden in a carefully selected spot for hours. As the sun began to dip in the west, deep shadows grew long on the dunes. The cooling sand rustled and Uri knew the wona was coming. He took his time and when the worm's head rose above the ground, Uri drove the grag's hook deep into the body. The wona flung itself up just once then collapsed on the sand, dead.

It was a good kill. Uri didn't even need the hook to pull the body from the depth of the sand.

Bibbi let out a loud whoop and they danced in circles. Then Uri examined the body, measuring it. It was fair size, almost three feet long.

After waving goodbye to Bibbi, he carried his trophy home, swinging the dead body across his shoulders for the entire village to see. Today he was a great hunter. It was his goal to be known someday as, "Uri the Great Hunter."

Through his village, nestled in the valley at the bottom of the sand dunes, he swaggered. He entered from the edge and walked down the main road.

Here the dirt path cut through the closely spaced mud houses. Some larger than others, but all made of the same material. The palm leaf roofs spread across his view like green waves, and the heat radiating from them rippled the air above. Few people were moving about at this time of the day. However, the ones he passed casually looked his way, and when they saw the wona he carried, they waved and nodded.

As Uri turned the corner, he entered the district where he lived, and came across a large wall. It separated the business stalls from the homes in that area. In this district, homes sat on larger plots of ground. The residents had room to grow the vegetables and fruit that sustained the village. The soil being poor, it was a meager living, but it was all they had.

Uri was not paying any attention to his surroundings at this point, so he didn't notice the boys above him on the wall. A taunting voice made him look up.

"Ooo, look at Uri. He got himself a big worm."

Rill, a golden haired, gangly boy, straddled the mud wall. Two other boys, all Uri's age, sat along side of Rill.

"Can we have some, pl-l-ease?" Rill pleaded in his unique sarcastic tone.

Uri stopped and glared at Rill. The boy swung down from the top of the wall to the dirt street and stood in front of

13

Uri, blocking his way. They were about the same height, Uri being stockier.

"Let me pass Rill," Uri uttered, low and threatening.

Rill circled Uri and poked at the dead wona. "Big deal." He said.

Uri pushed past. Continuing his way down the path, he saw Kerka at the end of the road watching the whole scenario.

"Hi Uri, I'm glad ya didn't let Rill push you around. You're so brave and gentle"

Blushing, Uri said, "Oh, he just talks big."

Kerka's hair was a blonde cloud that always seemed to need a good brushing, and despite obvious neglect by her parents, she always had a sunny smile. It reminded Uri of a spring day in the desert after one of the infrequent rains, a rainbow of hope and joy. Her eyes were the color of amber, like the liquid used by the healers of the village to cure many ills. Of all the children Uri thought Kerka was the nicest, and the cutest. However, she was only twelve, still a baby.

"Ya sure got a nice worm for your dinner." She fell in step with him. "Can I walk besides you for a while?"

"Sure, I guess so." Not wanting to admit, he was glad to have her company. He thought of sharing the wona, but there was really only enough for one family. This left him feeling sorry he hadn't caught a larger one, since most of the time Kerka's family did not have enough food. So, Uri decided he would bring some of his sister's vegetables to her house tomorrow, and that idea relieved his guilt.

"When can I go with ya out to the dunes?" Kerka asked as they reached the road where their paths would separate.

"You can't go out there with me." Uri told her.

"Why?"

14

"Because," he stopped and looked at her. "You're a girl."

"That's not an answer Uri. I want to go too. You're out there all the time." She put her hands on her hips.

"I go to be alone and think." He said, as if to end the subject, but Kerka continued.

Her eyes began to sparkle with wonder. "So, whatdya think about?"

"Mostly about why I'm here and what is my purpose. I think about why my parents died. Why we struggle for water when there is a big sea we can't drink from, and I wonder what is across that sea."

Kerka frowned. "The Dombaras are across the sea."

He squinted at the sun, low in the sky. "Sure, but what does that land look like?"

"Do you get any answers, Uri?"

"No I don't, but I keep asking." He waved goodbye and continued down the narrowing path to his home.

Chapter Three

Bibbi

The dunes sent elongated shadows across the valley floor. Bibbi approached the cave where his tribe had set up their encampment. He saw his father watching for him, and put his head down knowing he had been gone way too long. Now he had some explaining to do.

"Where have you been?" His father asked.

"I wanted to see what the sand dunes looked like."

"There was a very good reason you were told not to venture away from the compound. Did anyone see you?"

He couldn't tell his father about Uri so he stammered out a half-truth. "Be assured father, the Pinola tribe doesn't know we are here."

"You could have terminated our mission. We are leaving for home now." He looked at Bibbi, and said in a stern voice. "I'll deal with your disobedience later."

Bibbi wanted to ask him what the mission was, but he didn't dare push his father any further. He knew whatever discipline he received would be just, but waiting for it would be punishment enough, and his father knew it. He picked up his bedroll and joined the rest of the tribe as they waited to leave and return home.

Before the men shoved off in the boats, Bibbi saw his cousin, Coran, stand in front of them all. He was a disciple, priest, and prophet of the Creator. Coran's voice wafted over the shore as he offered a prayer for safekeeping of the men and their sons. They were in a cove by the cliffs of the Brown Hills, hidden from view, and Coran's prayer, short but intense, seemed to envelope the group in a protective shell.

Bibbi followed his Father as they climbed into one of the six large boats on the shore of the Green Sea. The older men and their sons equally filled two boats. Denola, the wife of Elder Pujim, stood at the helm of their boat. She was a formidable figure, a tall, large woman, and adept at sailing. She came from an important family in the tribe, and when necessary, often substituted in a man's position. Bibbi was afraid of her so he stayed close to his Father, wondering if he would ever see Uri again. He hoped so, because he had become quite fond of him.

The evening sky became a bluish-black as the boat responded to the winds and the waves. Bibbi watched the Pinola's land grow smaller. He was glad they soon would be home.

He sat in the dark next to his father as they sailed toward Dombara Land. Bibbi and the other boys traveled with the men as they hunted, and sailed around the land where they lived. However, they had never taken the children to the Pinola land before. Bibbi listen to the older men and his father talk.

"I think it was a mistake to bring the children with us this time. The mission is too dangerous."

"I agree," Said another. "However most of us thought it would be good for the boys to experience a different land."

"Well, I think it only made them curious about others and how they live. We should not be dragging them into this." Elajon said.

Bibbi looked up at his father, Elajon as he spoke and hoped he would not tell the others about his wanderings.

17

"Well, it was a mistake," the first man spoke again, "but then we all make mistakes."

"True, we are not perfect. We are always learning. The Creator forgives our blunders." Denola joined the conversation. The men nodded and murmured in agreement.

Bibbi snuggled up against his father. He was happy that only the two of them shared his secret of his wanderings, and enjoyed that safe feeling. His eyelids fluttered closed and despite his perplexing thoughts, he fell asleep.

It seemed only seconds had passed and they were home. Elajon shook Bibbi gently to waken him.

Bibbi rubbed his eyes, rising from the emptiness of sleep. "Are we home already?"

He saw his mother standing on the docks, holding his three-year-old sister, Sarella in her arms. Bibbi wanted to be held like that, but he was too old for that sort of thing. Tika, his older sister, now sixteen and ready for marriage, stared ahead looking to the other boat behind them. He knew she was looking for Koori, but he was not among the men returning. Bibbi wondered why the younger men stayed behind. What was their mission?

It was cold and dark as each boat emptied and everyone began walking home. The twin moons shone overhead, one waning more than the other. Bibbi didn't like the darkness that crept out at him from every corner so he stayed close to his mother.

It was a long walk, down the road by the shoreline. As they walked, the docks disappeared behind. They soon entered a clearing by the water. Bibbi, wide-eyed, looked into the dark, shadowy bushes scattered about, then seeing the stone house they lived in, he ran and entered. Now feeling safe and peaceful, Bibbi fell into his bed.

Chapter Four

Taken

When Uri arrived at the mud hut he called home, he could smell the comforting and familiar activities his sister did at this time of the day. Peeling the fresh vegetables and brewing the dark sweet drink, they enjoyed called Crost. Some Kavac milk would be there to lighten it a bit.

At the entrance stood the talisman, his sister Beka had put there years ago to keep evil spirits from entering their home. It was made of straw wound together with nuts from the Pokko tree. Dangling from that were several dried Jamic roots, bitter and poisonous. All together, it was around four feet high.

Uri had to bow down to enter because the entrance was small. The idea again was to keep spirits away. Beka and her husband Suwat met him, delighted with his catch. Since Suwat was lame, unable to provide for the family, Beka grew produce for the market.

They had lived on nothing but fruits and vegetables the last two weeks. Now Uri's worm assured strength and good health once again. Although the food they ate was fresh, straight from Beka's garden, they needed meat to stay healthy and strong.

The sun was gone from the horizon when he began roasting the wona. One by one, the evening sky displayed the flickering stars, but the twin moons would not appear until much later. Venca, which Uri learned meant The First, would rise with a rosy hue. Then moments later, the smaller, milky colored Visca, The Second, would peek from among the hills. Uri wondered what his new friend Bibbi was doing under the same dark sky. Waiting, as he was, for the soft light of the moons to bless the land with its comforting glow.

Beka prepared the small wooden table with fresh and bright colored vegetables, but in the center was a plate just for the sliced meat. Tonight Uri was happy. They ate greedily and soon the sparse remains of dinner were scattered about on the kitchen table. A flickering light of the lamp cast soft shadows as darkness crept around the home.

"Tell us again, Uri. Tell us how you killed the wona." Beka's dark eyes danced with excitement.

Uri smiled, and then looked very serious. "I waited, for a long time. Then I saw the head move."

"Hold on," said Suwat. "I'll be the wona.' He crossed the room and fell on the hard dirt floor.

"It lifted its head and I threw the grag." Uri swung his arm at Suwat.

Suwat fell back feigning death. They all laughed at his antics.

"Bibb--" Uri caught himself before he uttered Bibbi's name.

"What?" asked Beka.

Uri stopped, and then continued. "Beka, how did you do at market today?"

"Actually I sold out before noon." She stood and began to clear off the small table.

There was much joy in their home tonight, and they talked and joked while the evening grew late. They even discussed their parents, a painful subject. How life had been so difficult

20

after the accident, the fall that claimed their lives, and how things slowly got better.

It was past midnight, the High Hour, when Uri made his way to bed, a pallet in the back room. His room also consisted of a small wooden box where he kept his personal things. Next to the bed stood a small lamp, and a basin of water. He turned off the lamp and the house darkened as quiet filtered into the corners of the small rooms. Almost at once, sleep crept over him.

***

What was happening? Sleep was ripped from him. Shaken, confused and unable to see, Uri's mind struggled to grasp what was occurring right now. Someone yanked his hands behind him and tied them tight. He tried to open his mouth but a hand covered it.

He heard a voice in his left ear. "Don't be afraid. I will not hurt you. Just be quiet and everything will be fine."

A man dragged him across the floor. Wide-awake now, kicking and making as much noise as he could, Uri tried to get free, but he was small for his age and this man was tall and strong. Rough hands yanked him to the open door. He struggled to look at the man, but all he could see was his cloth covered legs, sandaled feet, and Dombara clothing. Uri looked down at the arm encircling him and noticed large, jagged scar running from the man's elbow to his wrist.

Twisting and writhing seemed to do no good, and the man again cautioned Uri.

"I am not going to hurt you, be still."

As they began to exit the hut, Uri looked back into the moonlit kitchen as Beka screamed.

"No! Let him go!" She flung herself on the man who was pulling Uri out the door.

21

The hand fell from Uri's mouth. "Beka, don't!" he cried, and struggled against the masked figure. "Leave her alone!"

She screamed again, but the assailant pushed her with his free hand, and she landed hard against the table. The table they had just been sitting at a few hours before, talking and laughing.

Uri watched his sister drop to the floor, motionless. Suwat limped into the chaos, his eyes widened with terror. He rushed to her crumpled body laying deadly still, tangled between the table legs.

Whisked from the house into the cool of the night, Uri saw chaos everywhere. Many children and masked figures ran in every direction.

"What are you doing?" He yelled at his abductor. "What's happening?" Anguish filled his throat like a fistful of sand. It spread down to his chest, falling as a burning fire into his stomach, like hot nesting coals.

He had no control over the circumstances, and the lack of power left him weak, dizzy, and disoriented. Someone threw a hood over his head and dropped him on what felt like a cart.

His fingers prodded the wide planks beneath him, rough and wooden. As the cart rocked back and forth, he felt the space all around him fill, as flesh pressed against flesh. Then he detected motion and heard the squeaking of wagon wheels. They must be going somewhere and fast.

All of this action took place in seconds, leaving Uri dazed and confused. The bonds on his wrists rubbed into the skin, and warm blood soon began to trickle into his palms. His legs cramped and the sound of sobbing filled his ears. Horrified, he realized children filled the cart. The motion began to agitate his back as it pressed against the side rails. Uri was never in his life so uncomfortable, so frightened, and so wretched.

They traveled down the wide road to the edge of the dunes and stopped.

Before they began the steep descent into the valley, the Dombara men removed the hoods and unloaded all of the children from the three carts. The men had been dragging the carts along the road, but now everyone had to walk.

The sounds of whimpering and sobbing filled the night air. Some of the older boys yelled and cursed at the Dombara men. Tied up, none of them could effectually run away. They could barely walk, but walk they did, down the road in the dark, at the command of the men.

As they reached the bottom of the valley, they came to the edge of the layered sandstone, the Brown Hills. Uri's wrists were numb but had stopped bleeding, his feet were sore. He had removed the foot bindings when he went to bed and, of course, had left them behind.

Questions occupied his mind. What had happened to Beka? What did these people want, and where were they all going?

When they came to the mouth of the caves many children became increasingly frightened, because of the legends of evil spirits told to them by their parents. Wondering if they were to be eaten, or attacked by devils, the younger ones cried and began to cling to the older ones. Yet, in spite of their protests, the men forced them all into the gaping entry and directed them to sit against the walls.

"It's going to be Okay." Uri weakly assured those around him.

He too was frightened, and he heard his heart pounding in his ears. Then it came to him. This was the mission of the Dombara patrol, to kidnap the children. But why, and for what purpose?

Guilty nausea washed over him. Uri knew the Dombaras were here and had said nothing. Selfishly he had enjoyed making a new friend and showing off for him. His sister may be dead, and he had betrayed her. Overcome with grief, Uri hung his head and joined the sobbing that echoed all around him. What was to become of them all?

Chapter Five

Departure

The air, the ground, everything felt close and clammy. Darkness prevented Uri from seeing much of his surroundings. Even the torches, placed in a single row into the depth of the cave, projected only ghostly flickers of pale light against the walls. He could feel the cold unyielding rock against his back, and he smelled a grimy quality to the stale air, as if evil vapors emitted from the ground.

As his eyes became accustomed to the darkness, Uri looked at the children sitting side by side against both walls of the cave. Uri had never seen the inside of a cave, and he didn't like it. It felt oppressive and was very, very dark.

"Hey, Uri." A voice came from the opposite side. "Over here,"

Uri squinted into the dark. "Is that you Rill?"

"Yah, do you know what's happened?"

Guilt caused his answer to be gruff and quick. "No. Why would I know?"

"I just wondered. Look, this place is filled with all the kids from our village."

Rill wasn't so cocky now, but his sarcastic tongue still flashed. "Uri, you're so smart, what do you think they're going to do with us?"

Uri ignored the question. He saw a small figure starting toward him. It was Kerka. She was very frightened and her cheeks stained with tears. She pushed in next to him.

"I want my mother." She began to sob.

He knew there would be no rescue, so Uri said nothing to her. No Pinola men would venture down into this valley or into the caves. The fear of evil spirits kept them away. He thought the Dombaras were a peaceful tribe, like the Pinolas. The tribes near his village, the Yokas and Rabirs, never caused any problems. They all traded goods and respected each other's territories.

Uri thought they also had the same beliefs about the spirits that ruled the land. Evidently, the Dombaras did not hold that belief. Bibbi said there wasn't anything in these caves and Uri didn't see anything either. He was at a loss to understand what was happening. No one knew much about this tribe from across the sea.

"Hey," Rill yelled at one of the Dombara men walking past. "I gotta get home. You better let me go." The man walked by without turning his head.

"Hey you, look at me." Rill seemed desperate. "Uri, you tell 'em. Come on Uri, you're big and bad."

Still Uri didn't answer. His heart ached for Beka. She looked so white and still, lying under the table where she had fallen from the man's attack. She didn't deserve such cruel treatment. His sister worked hard, hauling buckets of water to the small garden she tended, coaxing shoots to grow from the poor, sandy soil, standing all day at the market where she sold those vegetables to provide for himself and Suwat. As Uri thought of the loving family he would be leaving behind, grief enveloped him.

"Hey, we gotta get outa here." Rill's voice brought Uri back to the frightening situation they faced. "I need to help my mother this morning."

Several Dombara men began to walk between the rows of children. Each one stopped at a child to look at the bottom of their right foot, then wrote something on a pad. They would go to another and repeat the same thing.

Uri grew alarmed and frightened. He knew he had a mark on his heel. He was told to keep it covered, because people might think it was a mark from an evil spirit. That is why he always wore his foot bindings. Uri felt shame as the men approached, knowing they would discover his secret. He feared the man who looked at his foot would cry out, and maybe hurt him.

He watched the men approach Rill and the other boys, and choked back tears so Rill wouldn't see his reaction. They began to kick and yell, but the men were quick to overpower them. Uri began to wonder if the other boys also had marks?

He was next and panic resulted in his whole body curling up, and his heart pound against his chest. There was nothing he could do. The Dombara grabbed Uri's squirming feet, and he waited for some kind of a reaction. The man just calmly continued writing and went to the next child. Uri looked at him in amazement.

Turning to Kerka, next to him, Uri said, "Let me see your foot."

He saw fear in her eyes as she shook her head.

"Do you have a mark on it?"

"Please, don't ask." She whimpered.

"Do you have a mark?" Uri persisted.

"Yes." She cried big tears as she lifted her foot.

He saw several black markings, different from his, but strikingly alike. His mouth dropped. "Oh!" His mind whirled. "Were you told never to show anyone?"

She nodded and continued to sob. Uri leaned close to her. If he hadn't been tied up, he would have hugged her. Even so, the sobbing quieted.

Uri was still reeling from the commotion involving everyone's feet when he noticed an older Dombara standing in front of the mouth of the cave. He was tall and dressed differently from the rest. The other men wore beaded vests, but this man had many decorations, feathers, and a headband of beads. The other men had finished their inspection, but were still writing on the pads.

"My name is Elder Pujim. I am in charge here." His voice rang clearly through the cave. "You will not be harmed so do not be afraid. We are taking you home."

The children became excited, thinking they were to be released.

"Quiet." Pujim waited for a moment. "We are taking you across the Green Sea. Now line up in two straight rows. You will be getting aboard the boats immediately."

A loud cry of objection went up, but they were hustled out of the cave with their hands still tied. The younger ones had their hands tied in front, the older ones, in back, disabling them more. No one had time to think or react. The men carried some of the smaller ones, and shoved the rest. Uri never realized how close the water was to the caves

Rill and Uri ended up on different boats. The Dombaras separated the six older boys, and Uri huddled next to younger boys and girls. Kerka sat at the stern of the boat. She held onto another girl the same age. They were shivering and their faces wet with tears. She turned and looked at him, opened her mouth to say something, but Uri shook his head. It would not be wise to divulge who knew whom.

Elder Pujim was at the front and within the sound of Uri's voice, but Uri sat silently for a long while as they sailed from his home. The wind howled and tossed the boats around in the cold sea.

Anger and a sour hatred began to fill Uri's mouth. He had to say something. He could not sit here against his will, so he screamed into the wind.

"What do you think you're doing, taking us like slaves away from our families?"

Pujim ignored him. His grey braid was long and whipped about in the wind. He stood with his back straight, strong, and fierce. His craggy face was blank, showing no emotion. His dark, amber eyes did not disclose any thoughts.

Uri strained forward to get as close to the old man as possible, twisting his bound hands, and kicking his feet in frustration. "We have a right to know what you're doing."

"So you do, young man." Pujim did not look at Uri, but watched the waves from the sea buffet the front of the boat. "You are being taken home."

The clouds parted and one of the moons shone an eerie, pale light onto the face of the old Dombara man. Frightening thoughts of evil spirits and ghosts flashed across Uri's confused mind, but he quickly recovered. "My home is back there. You're kidnapping us."

The Elder turned and looked directly into Uri's eyes. "We are undoing a great wrong." Then he stood over Uri, rocking as the boat pitched in the water. "Be quiet, for you are frightening the little ones."

Amazed at the gentleness of the elder's voice, Uri stopped. He had expected anger, and perhaps some abusive action, but not gentleness and concern. Uri put his head down and shivered as the damp wind from the sea whipped across the boat. The man turned and stoically looked ahead at the land growing larger in the distance.

29

Uri looked too, getting the first sight of his destination, the land of the Dombara's.

Chapter Six

Arrival

The rising sun sent golden waves across the emerald hills that lined the edge of the horizon. As they sailed closer, Uri saw the landscape was quite breathtaking. The color green was everywhere, on the ground, the trees, and over all the hills. It was an amazing sight, just as Bibbi described. There were no signs of sand or dunes.

Two platforms started at the edge of the sea, and as the boats moved into them, Uri studied buildings and the houses lining the shore, all made from blocks of rock, nothing like the mud dwellings he lived in.

The boats docked side by side, and everyone disembarked. They all stood shivering in the cold morning air. None of the children were dressed for this cooler weather. They all had on their light sleeping garments, and were barefoot.

Men came around and untied everyone's hands. Uri rubbed his wrists wondering what would happen now. He looked for Rill and saw him on the other side of the far platform. The Dombara men quickly herded them up a walkway that led to a large building.

It was bright and warm inside, furnished with long tables and chairs in rows. It reminded Uri of school. As the children entered the room, they cowered next to the walls, huddling together in groups. The whimpering and sobbing began again. They all were tired and frightened.

31

Uri watched several older women emerge from behind the platform and spread out among the smaller children, talking to them in a soothing voice. It seemed to comfort them. Some women sat on the floor and held the little ones in their laps. This simple act quieted them, and soon the women coaxed them to sit at the tables. Older Dombara children mingled with the other Pinola children. One boy came up to Uri.

"My name is Vail, what's yours?"

"Uri."

"Welcome to our village."

Uri glared at him, but said nothing. He could see this whole scenario was planned very well.

The children began to mix and gather in groups, and as they began to chatter and whisper to each other, Uri could see, they weren't as frightened once joined with friends. The grandmotherly women disappeared, along with the other Dombara children.

Uri sat down at the closest table to the doorway. As the moments went by anger grew, and replaced any leftover fear. He became sullen, his eyes moving across the room, looking at everyone. He saw Kerka with a girl her own age. They seemed to be gradually losing their fear, and began to tolerate these indignities.

Rill came over and sat across from him. "What can we do? The kids are not afraid anymore, why aren't they trying to get away?"

"For the same reason you aren't. They don't know what to do or where to go, so they don't do anything." Uri shook his head. "Look, most of them are sitting and talking as if nothing bad happened."

Women appeared carrying trays of dishes, bowls, and cups. The tables filled with large quantities of food. There were soft round things, yellow chucks of curds, patties of strange smelling meats, and oddly shaped fruits.

"Breakfast," Uri thought, disgusted that his mouth began to water. He decided he would not touch any of this foreign garbage.

"Hey, at least they are going to feed us, looks good, huh?"

Uri glared at Rill and wanted to rebuke him for accepting this offering, but just then a voice boomed across the large room, and everyone quieted down. Uri turned and there was a Dombara man, standing on the platform in front of them.

"We know you are all hungry, tired, and cold. We have prepared food for you that is probably strange."

Uri sniffed, "He can say that again."

"Please, try it all. The eggs are very good, and the meat is cooked just the way you like."

"Eggs, what kind of eggs?" Uri said.

Rill just shrugged his shoulders.

The only eggs Uri knew of were the wona's, and they were hard, rubbery, and inedible.

"There are pitchers of milk on the tables. You may have all you like."

A woman came forward dressed in a long, colorful gown. Her golden hair piled high on her head and held there with a beaded clasp. "After breakfast you will be taken to an area where you can wash and clean up. Boys on one side, girls on the other." She pointed behind the platform. "Warmer clothing will be there for you to dress in. In addition, there are sandals for your feet. Then you will come back here. Further instructions will be given at that time."

She backed up and vanished behind a door, and Uri was left to ponder the food. He picked up one of the soft, round things, scrutinized it from all angles, and reluctantly put it on the dish in front of him.

"That is a biscuit." A young woman smiled as she passed by with a pitcher of milk. "It's made from flour, eggs, and butter."

He knew about milk and butter, but eggs again. The thought of hard rubbery eggs like the wona's took away his appetite. Rill tasted a few things, but the others around them ate hardily.

Uri watched Rill's wide, angular face and grimaced. "How could you eat this weird food?"

"Well, I have to admit, I'm hungry. So if they offer it, I might as well."

The boy next to Uri gulped down a tall glass of milk.

"It's all good." He offered up a glass but Uri just sat frowning and looked away. He left the biscuit in front of him untouched. The children were eating and chatting as if nothing was wrong. He shook his head. This was not right.

Rill's hunger was evidently satisfied and he pushed himself back from the table. "I've gotta find a way to get home, Uri, right away. My mother needs me."

"Why are you so concerned about your mother? We all need to get home."

"But I have to gather Cacarus for her." Rill's eyes changed as sadness began to creep in.

"That spiny thing that grows out in the back desert?" Uri knew of the plant, but why was Rill interested in it?

He nodded. "We shred and dry the outer-side and she pulls it into thick strands. It's great for baskets. She weaves

34

baskets from it, and that's the way we make money to survive."

Rill's hands curled up into balls and he pounded on the table. "I have to help her. She is too weak to do it herself. She will die if I do not get home. Uri, I've got to leave." He leaned forward, his eyes now intent and angry. "You have to help me."

Before Uri could answer, Rill pushed himself away from the table and rushed to the area behind the platform.

Chapter Seven
How to Get Home

Uri continued to think how to escape as he filed out with the other children to wash and change clothes. He stopped with others at a pile of shirts and long pants. The clothing was strange, as everything else had been. He picked up a pair of pants, and a soft, thick shirt. Reluctantly, Uri changed into the warmer clothes. He rolled up the long sleeves of the shirt, and put on the sandals. He was grateful for those, because his feet were very sore.

Uri found a jar of salve among the provided articles, and rubbed it on his raw wrists. Also he wash the dried blood from his hands. He walked past the other boys who were changing, listening to what they were saying.

"Hey, this ain't so bad."

"Yah, they gave us food and they haven't been mean or anything."

Uri sighed. Tired of their complacent attitude, he turned and yelled at them all. "Don't you want to go home? Have you already forgotten your parents, your families? What is the matter with you?"

Someone in the middle of the crowed room yelled back, "How do we go home?" "Yah, how do we get across the sea, swim?" Others snickered and began to shout all at once.

"Well," Uri thought to himself, *"I guess it doesn't matter to me if they're not afraid anymore".*

Then from behind him, he heard a voice. "We want to go home." Uri turned and saw two boys standing with Rill.

"Good," Uri said. At last there might be a way. "Now we have to stay together. We can cause a lot of trouble, but only if we stay together."

The tall one Uri knew as Dron. He had been sitting with Rill on the wall. The other, he heard Rill call him Jai. These three seemed to Uri, determined and single-minded, however they couldn't talk anymore for now everyone began to gather in another room.

The next phase of this "Indoctrination," as Uri named, it was a cozy storytelling time. They had been ushered into a smaller building, with a warm fire burning in a corner area. The Dombara men and women instructed everyone to sit on the floor, cross-legged and listen to a story.

Nodding to Rill and the other boys to follow him into the back of the room, Uri saw this as a good opportunity to start a rebellion. Uri thought the four of them showed a respectable force. They stood with their arms folded, looking very determined. This did not go unnoticed by the adults. A few wandered back to them and pointed to the benches.

"You boys can sit here, if you wish."

"We don't wish." Uri spat back.

"I understand how you feel." One of the older men put his hand on Rill's shoulder, but Rill shrugged it off.

"We want you to feel comfortable, but if you make it hard the little ones will be frightened."

"Sit and listen, please, for their sake." Another spoke quietly.

37

Rill was the first to succumb to the reasoning. The others followed, but Uri stood firm.

The first man to speak stood close to Uri, so close he could feel the heat from his body. "That's Okay. If you want to be different go to the head of the room, and sit next to the teacher. He won't mind."

Uri smiled to himself. That was a good idea. So taking his time, he swaggered, just enough to look tough, and stood behind the teacher. The handsome man was taller than the others, and held himself with confidence. He turned and greeted Uri with a friendly smile.

"Hi, what is your name, young man?"

"Uri. In my home I am known as a great hunter." Inside Uri began to tremble. Perhaps he had gone too far.

"Oh, that's great, Uri. You look like a hunter, big and very strong. Say, could you do me a favor." He leaned close to speak softly. "You see those boys in the back?"

Uri looked at his companions.

"I think they might need someone like yourself, you know, brave and fearless. I think you are a good leader. The smaller children need to look up to you older ones." He stopped and winked. "I need you to keep an eye on them. Would you help me by doing this favor?"

Uri knew they duped him. Yet despite his reluctance to back down, he chose to comply with the man's request, this time. He sundered to the back with a sheepish look on his face, and sat next to the boys.

Chapter Eight
The Story

Now that Uri and the boys were sitting and listening, the teacher began the story.

"A long, long time ago a tribe of people lived in this land, by the Green Sea. They were peaceful, happy, and made by the Creator of All."

Uri blinked. What was this Creator of All? He wanted to know more about this being, but the storyteller continued without explanations.

"There came a time when some of them wanted to move, and find a different way to live. After many years, the people spread out to other lands, and several different tribes began to emerge. They all stayed separate and called themselves by different names. Still, everyone was peaceful. No wars, no invasions, no major trouble of any kind. These tribes became our tribes, the Pinola and the Dombara and others you may know about."

All eyes stayed glued to the storyteller.

"Then fourteen years ago our people were invaded in the middle of the night, robbing us of the most important thing we owned. We didn't know whom or where the invasion came from. The invaders stole our boats, knowing we would be unable to follow them.

We weren't warriors, we didn't know how to fight, and we had no weapons. However, we went to the tribes in our land and inquired among them. We believed they told the truth and knew nothing about the invasion. So... we accepted our loss, and after grieving, we went on with our lives. Two years later in the middle of the night, it happened again. More loss, more grieving. Now we knew we had to find out where these people were from, and why they did this.

We went again to the tribes in our land. They assured us they had no information.

Wondering if it came from across the sea, we set up sentries around the docks and in the village. The Council of Elders began to discuss traveling across the sea, but they could not agree on a plan. The elders bogged down with ponderous debates so nothing got accomplished. We continued to watch and guard our village.

Then three years passed. We hoped it was over, but they attacked again. This time we were ready, but the enemy was fierce, and many people were hurt. They succeeded in robbing us again, but now we knew who they were. We knew it was the Pinola Tribe. We sent spies into their land to see what happened to the precious property they had stolen. We found our precious property was safe, but it belonged to us. We wanted it back. The elders of our village finally came to an agreement. First, we sent an emissary of six men to confer with the other tribe's elders. They listened to us, but they did not admit anything. They did promise to check into our accusations and return their findings and decision. A year went by. We never heard from them. Our patience was our weakness."

He stopped and paused for a few seconds. The children leaned forward, enthralled with the story.

"Do you want to know what they stole?"

"Yes, tell us." The response came from all over the room. Even Uri, Rill and the other boys joined in the chorus.

The storyteller sat back. "Our precious property that the tribe from across the sea stole from us, was our babies and our infants."

A gasp rose from the group of thirty-two children. The implication of these words was not lost on Uri. Realizing the oldest among them was fourteen, he knew where they were going with this story. An icy trepidation enveloped him.

"Yes, our children," he continued. "We were hesitant to attack the Pinola tribe because we were afraid the children might get hurt. Many were still so young. The elders continued to argue among themselves and they made no decisions. Sadly, it happened once more, five years ago. A terrible fight ensued and we fought them off, but they did manage to steal four more. They got away with four more babies. Now we knew it had to stop. We began to devise a plan to get everyone back."

Suddenly Rill's face went white. He looked at Uri. Then he stood up with his mouth open. "That's us!" He cried and sat back down stupefied.

"No it's not!" Uri whispered loudly. "They're lying."

The man continued. "We waited until the last four babies were older and we felt we could go in and take all the children without injuring anyone."

Uri stood and pointed an accusing finger at the storyteller. "People were injured, my sister for one. This is all a lie. What do you really want?"

Some children began to cry, and it appeared the meeting would dissolve into chaos. In order to restore control, the men moved among the children to quiet them.

The storyteller cried out. "Wait, children wait. We know who belongs to us. We have a way of identifying our own. Look at your feet. You all bear our tattoo. The family name is on the heels of all our children. All of you have a tattoo. Not only do we know you belong to us, we know which family you came from."

There was immediate dead silence in the room. Not one of the children moved or reacted in any way. The adults waited for the information to make an impression on their young minds. Uri knew it wasn't that they didn't understand. They didn't know how to react. They didn't know what to do.

Uri spoke first. "You think because you say we were born here, you own us and we should believe you?"

"Yah." Dron spoke next. "Maybe all the tribes tattoo their babies."

The storyteller stood and looked over the room. "The truth has been spoken here. You all belong to families here in this village. Your mothers and fathers still grieve over you. Of course they want you back."

Rill jumped to his feet, his face red with rage. "My mother is back home, across the sea. I don't have any other mother but her."

Uri joined in. "This whole story is a lie. You want us to believe it so you can keep us here for... for a reason."

The Elder Pujim stepped in front of the group, and held up his hand for quiet. His piercing stare covered the room. His very presence initiated calm, and the boys sat down.

"Try to understand children. Your real parents love you, and will be here soon for you. Please give us a chance." He looked around, "You are here now." Then with cold deliberateness, he added. "And here you will stay."

Uri turned to Rill and whispered. "Just wait, don't do anything now. Just wait. We will go home."

Most of the children sat in stunned silence, waiting for the next event to happen. It was immediate and rapid. Several Dombara women guided the children to a large, wide corridor, and slowly strangers came to whisk them away. At that moment, Uri saw Kerka running toward him. Her face was flushed and her eyes wide with apprehension. The shirt provided to all the twelve-year-olds hung down, almost to her knees. Uri never realized before how small she was.

"Wait." She stood next to him, looking up with such hopefulness.

"You were so brave, standing up to those men. Do you think they will let us go home now?"

Sadness tightened around Uri's heart. She was innocent, so young for her twelve years. There was no helping himself or anyone, right now. He hesitated, looking into her wide, frightened eyes. Underneath, dark circles told the story of constant hunger, and lack of care.

"No, they won't let us go home just yet." He saw a couple walking towards them. "I'm afraid you will have to go with these people here." He nodded at them.

Kerka's chin began to tremble, and large tears rolled down her face.

Uri put his hands on her shoulders. "It's all right and don't be afraid. Go with them. They won't hurt you." Then he whispered, "I'll find where you are and come see you, soon as I can."

She clung to his arm with her thin, white fingers. The couple smiled at them both and the woman extended her hand.

"I'll go if you say so." Kerka's fingers loosened the tight grip, and she turned to face the couple.

"Go on, I'll see you soon."

Uri watched as she took the hand of the woman, and walked away without looking back. This was so cruel and humiliating. Anger filled him. He felt violated, helpless and frustrated, all at the same time. Yet an uncomfortable nagging pulled at him. What was this tattoo thing all about?

Chapter Nine

Surprise

The sun rose in the east, spilling its color and warmth over the Dombara homeland, and into the open window where Bibbi lay on his bed, enjoying the soft, comfort compared to the rough pad he slept on for several days in the damp cave. Then he remembered the coming punishment and the enjoyment vanished.

It wasn't long before his father's voice echoed into his room from the kitchen. Soon the bedroom doorway filled with Elajon's tall figure.

"Bibbi, get up and come to breakfast."

"Yes Father." He quickly dressed, and slipped into his sandals next to the door.

There was an abundance of sounds and smells in the kitchen. Fresh cooked eggs and pieces of fruit took center stage on the table, while hot biscuits piled high in a colorful basket.

Bibbi's mother filled his cup with milk from a pitcher and handed it to Tika.

"Thank you." He said weakly, waiting for the stern voice of his father.

"Bibbi, do you know what happened last night?"

45

"No." He took a large drink from his cup, and looked from Tika back to his father.

"Listen to me." Elajon said. "Our mission in Pinola land was to bring back the children that had been stolen from us, over the years."

Bibbi and Tika stared at their father. His sister gasped and covered her mouth.

"Four times in the last fourteen years the Pinolas came across the sea and stole the babies, and newborns. We had one taken from us. Now he is back."

Bibbi continued staring. He did not understand what his father was saying.

"Young man, are you ready to tell me where you went during the days we were in the Pinola land?"

"Uh... yes." He involuntarily jerked, knowing he had to tell them about meeting Uri. "I wanted to see what the sand dunes were like, and I met a Pinola boy hunting a wona, a big worm."

"Did he know who you were?"

"Yes, he saw the patrol down in the valley." Then added quickly, "But he didn't tell anyone. He told me it was our secret."

"Now why would he do that?" Elajon asked, suspicious.

"Simple, we liked each other." Bibbi answered, shrugging his shoulders.

"What was this boy's name?"

"Uri."

His father's face dropped. "Oh my!"

"What's wrong?" Marga, the mother looked alarmed.

46

Instead of answering her Elajon learned over to Bibbi. "Your punishment will be that you will go to the compound alone, and find this boy, Uri. Bring him home to us. Do you understand me?"

"Yes Father."

Then Elajon turned to his wife. "Uri is Niliab."

Bibbi watched his mother's face turn white. She sat down, hard.

"Bibbi," Elajon continued, "Uri is your brother."

Chapter Ten

Taken Home

All the children were leaving with their supposed newfound family members. Uri left the spot where he watched Kerka walk away, and went to join Rill and Jai standing against the back wall. They shuffled about waiting for what, they did not know. A large family group stood some distance from the three boys. They were watching, hesitant to move. At the lead was an impressive-looking man. Behind him were three young men, and a small girl. The man smiled kindly at Jai and beckoned to him.

"I guess this is it." Jai sighed and stepped forward. The man met him halfway, put his large hands on Jai's shoulders as tears formed in his eyes. Uri looked over to see Rill's reaction, and when he looked back up, someone he recognized was coming through the crowds, heading straight at him.

Uri saw Bibbi at a distance and almost called his name aloud. The eight-year-old walked up, stood in front of them, and looked uneasy. His eyes stopped at Uri.

"I w-was sent to bring you home." Bibbi quickly took Uri's hand and led him toward the outside door.

Uri wanted to run, but where could he go and where could he hide? He didn't know this land. Looking down into Bibbi's face, the familiar smile that captivated Uri on the dunes, quieted his fears. How long ago was that? It seemed like years. Unable to change the situation, he squeezed Bibbi's hand and went with him.

"Hey Uri," cried Rill. "Find me. Look till you find me."

Uri yelled over his shoulder, "I will. Trust me. I will."

At that moment an older man and woman walk toward Rill. He watched Rill stiffen as they reached out to touch him.

Rill pushed them away. "Get way from me."

"Please son, we are here to take you home. You are our son."

Rill began to swing his arms wildly. "No you aren't. My mother is across the sea. I don't know you, and I will not go anywhere with you!"

Uri looked at Bibbi, both of them surprised at the outburst.

Again, the older couple tried to reason with Rill, but now he was in a tantrum mode. Two large Dombara men ran up and held on to Rill, trying to calm him down.

Uri knew he could help. He ran back to where the commotion was going on.

"Rill, listen to me, it's Uri. Listen!"

Rill's face was red and his eyes wide, but Uri's voice seemed to reach him, and he stopped struggling.

"Do what they say now. I'll talk to you later."

Rill's glazed eyes turned to Uri's. "Huh?"

"Go with these people now and relax. I'll talk to you soon."

Rill's eyes were wet, but Uri's could see he was struggling not to cry.

"Can you hear and understand me?" Uri asked.

"Yah, I'll go."

Rill, in a daze slowly followed the couple out the door.

"Wow," Uri sighed, turning back to Bibbi. "I feel sorry for those people. They will have a real problem with him."

Then Uri and Bibbi went out the door and into the bright morning, a morning that had turned into a nightmare.

They walked together back down the path Uri had come when brought to the Community Building. Nearing the shore, Uri followed Bibbi as he turned down the path that past the stone houses, headed to a family that insisted he belonged to them.

Bibbi walked along, silent. They passed many houses where people were celebrating, welcoming children to what they were calling home. He saw strange and unusual animals in some backyards. He wanted to ask Bibbi what they were, but words would not form. He felt confused. Where was he going?

At last, they came to the edge of a cluster of homes. In front of him was a house like all the rest except a wooden fence surrounded the land it sat on. Bibbi stopped and motioned for Uri to go up the walk. The door opened, and the moment he entered the house strange faces met his.

Uri could feel the strong emotions from these people filling every corner of the room where he stood. These emotions entered uninvited, and crept through his mind. He waited, not daring to speak, because things would come out of his mouth he did not want expressed. He let them speak first.

"We welcome you home." The father said tentatively. "This is your birth family." He introduced each one to Uri. "Your mother."

He looked at a trembling woman with tears in her eyes.

50

"Your sisters Tika, little Sarella, and I believe you know Bibbi."

Uri glanced from face to face.

Then finding words he said, "Are you joking? I don't know any of you. I don't believe any of this--- this kidnapping all the babies, this story. Why are you doing this?"

The mother gasped and broke out in sobs, running from the room. Uri didn't care. His mind could not wrap around the events of the last few hours.

"I understand this is hard for you, Uri. Actually, your name really is Niliab –"

Uri broke into the father's explanations. "No, my name is Urikael. I am named after my father and I am called Uri."

By now, Bibbi and Tika were also crying.

"Well," the father began again. "You were born to us fourteen years ago, and the Pinolas really did steal you from us. Now you are home, back to stay. Your name is Niliab and we will call you that."

Uri knew any further arguments were useless. Although he was seething inside, he was quiet. Elajon brought him to a bedroom he would share with Bibbi. He had new clothing and brush for his hair. The father said if he needed anything else to ask for it. He silently sat on the edge of the bed, looking as defiant as possible, and stared at the man who was calling himself his father.

If Uri could have run anywhere to get away, he would have, but there was nowhere to run. He was here, captive in a strange land, surrounded by strange people, and powerless to do anything. His head began to ache and nausea filled his belly.

He would bide his time. There would eventually be a chance to escape. It had to come sometime, but until then he had to play along with this masquerade.

Chapter Eleven
A New Family

It was early dawn. The clouds on the horizon blushed with a rosy hue as the sun rose in the eastern sky. For days, Uri watched as those clouds emitted rain on the other side of the window. Dampness was not a good feeling for Uri. He longed for the deep golden waves of the sand dunes, the heavy heat of the streaming sun, and a cloudless, blue sky.

Uri turned over and sat his chin on the windowsill. He was used to spending his time outside in the dunes and the surrounding desert of his home. However, today was another day in this awful place that was not his home. The trees grew thick in the forest behind the house. Everything was green, an uncomfortable color which did not seem natural to Uri. Add to that a grey dripping sky, he quickly became depressed. In addition, a deep, homesick feeling was growing as the days passed.

Dark, troubling thoughts consumed him. The parents discreetly kept him in the house. Seven whole days he sat in the confines of these walls, while strange people watched him, trying to talk and reach him with their wants and feelings. Did he really have another name, a brother, and other sisters? He was tired of hearing it and wanted to believe they were lying.

He longed only for Beka and Suwat. What had happened to them? Were they trying to find him, or did they accept his capture and continue their lives without him? Most of all he worried if Beka had survived that terrible fall. He hadn't been able to look for Rill, Dron, Jai, or any of the others. Someone in the family was with him every minute, either the couple that claimed to be his parents or Tika.

Bibbi walked into the room, crawled up on his own bed, across from Uri's, and sat cross-legged at the end. "How would you like to take a walk today?"

Uri sat up. "Yeh."

"Mother said I could take you over to the play field this morning."

Mother, he sneered, a woman that fawned over him. Every time he looked at her, she had tears in her eyes. He didn't want this family, and he desperately wanted to return home, his real home.

Then Uri thought of the marks on his foot. "Bibbi, come here. Let me see the bottom of your feet."

Obediently Bibbi came over and sat near Uri on the bed. As he picked up his feet, Uri saw the tattoo on the bottom of his right foot. He studied it. "What do those marks mean?"

"The top one is my name Bibbi, then under that is our family name, Yaro.

And the last mark is the location where all the information can be found in the public records."

"Can you read mine?" Uri showed Bibbi his foot and for the first time felt no embarrassment.

"Sure. It says, Niliab. That is your name now. The rest says Yaro, 4756-2 North."

"Bibbi, do you think, since we all came from the same origins, everyone has a tattoo?"

Bibbi thought for a while." No, because I never saw a tattoo on any of the Mudans." Referring to the eastern tribe.

54

Uri never saw one on Beka or Suwat either. *"If this is a lie, how can I explain the tattoo"?* He thought.

"Come on Niliab," Bibbi called him by the name given to him at his arrival. Let's have breakfast and go play."

"I'm too old to play Bibbi, but I do want to go for a walk." He punched his brother's arm, gently, because he really loved this little guy. He could not deny the strong feelings.

They went to the kitchen area together where breakfast was underway.

Tika looked up at Uri as she brushed back the blond curls from her face. Hesitating, she glanced down. "Are you learning to like the eggs?" She asked, keeping her eyes on her plate.

Uri did like the eggs. He learned they came from what they called an Ovi, a rather large bird, kept in cages behind the house. He thought how weird they looked, strutting about, scratching and clawing at the ground while all the time making a strange clucking sound.

"Yes, actually I do." He admitted and sat in his designated chair. "But don't give me any of that meat, just a biscuit," he added, "please."

"Niliab," the mother touched his shoulder. "Bibbi will show you the play field at the park today. It's over near the school where all of you will be going to in three weeks." She smiled.

"Yeh, he told me already." Uri answered with a flat tone to his voice. He heard a sigh emit from her, but didn't react to it. He vacillated between wanting not to be rude, and wanting to reject their attention.

He thought, *"Just finished my food, get outside into the fresh air and away from them all."*

Uri was elated to leave the confines of the house and walk. It didn't matter where. He heard strange bird songs coming from the trees while he and Bibbi ambled along on the level path. He could see all around him. In the distance, groups of people walked to and from different pathways. As they left the homes behind, a meadow stretched before them. The sun was warm and it had stopped raining, so the air felt drier and comfortable. It was going to be a better day.

It was a short distance to the park and play field. Uri felt energized by stretching his legs and moving along the path. Little Bibbi had to run just to keep up.

They entered an area surrounded by trees and bushes. Benches crouched here and there, for sitting and relaxing, and bubbling fountains seemed located at equal distances surrounding the park.

At the far end, there was an area of sand for little ones to play in, and at the opposite side, a large open area where several children Bibbi's age were kicking around what resembled a large sock, tightly stuffed with Ovi feathers.

Bibbi pointed, "There, those are my friends." "My friends are over there on the Cho field."

Uri watched as Bibbi ran to join them. He had spotted Rill sitting on a bench by thick bushes, close to a trickling stream. Uri walked over to him, glancing back at Bibbi who was now involved in the game with his friends.

"Uri... am I glad to see you. Don't you hate all this wet weather?"

"Yeh, it rains all the time." Uri sighed, "Gosh, it's good to hear my real name." What name did they give you?"

"I don't wanna tell you, it's embarrassing."

"Don't be stupid, tell me."

"It's Pon." Rill hung his head, "Sounds like one of those bugs back home."

"That's a Pron." Uri snickered. He visualized the ugly, furry creature with six legs that let off a putrid smell, and leaked green ooze when touched.

"Mine is Niliab." It came out from between his teeth. "At first I ignored them when they called me that, but then I realized it would only be for a little while. I might as well keep it peaceful, besides, we are going home soon."

"Yah, when? I've been looking all over for you. Those people I live with drive me crazy."

"I bet you are doing your best to do the same to them."

"Huh?" Rill didn't get it.

Uri let it drop and continued. "I was only able to get away this morning. We need to meet tonight when there's no one around," Uri whispered, casting an anxious glance at Bibbi. "Get back here tonight, late, after the second moon rises." Uri quickly calculated that would be about an hour before midnight. "Can you do that?"

"I think so, sure." Rill answered.

Uri looked again toward Bibbi, and then his eyes turned toward the area where the sea began, past the horizon. "We need to get a boat. Steal one or something."

"They guard the docks all day and all night. I was down there last night snooping around and…"

Uri put his face close to Rill. "Are you trying to get away without me?"

"No, no. I was just wandering around, that's all."

Uri thought, *"Puny, lying coward, you are a Pron"*. Just because Rill was friendly didn't mean they were now buddies, and Uri knew he would double-cross him in a heartbeat.

"Don't ever try to go without me." Uri didn't know what made him angrier, Rill's lies or the ability to provoke this intense fury he felt.

Jai walked up at that moment. "Hey, what's going on?"

"Did you go down to the docks too?" Uri glared at Jai.

"No."

Uri glowered at him, feeling his eyes burning into bright orange flames, his lips pulled back over his teeth. "Don't lie to me."

"What's the problem here?" Jai whispered, looking around to see if anyone was watching. The noise from the children playing masked their voices.

"If anyone runs away, they will start watching us even closer. Then no one else will be able to leave. I'm getting out of here. Either we go together or no one goes."

"Okay, Uri. We go together." Rill agreed.

"I'll see you tonight." Uri looked at both of them and walked back to watch Bibbi play. His anger dissipated, but he was suspicious and distrustful of both Rill and Jai.

Chapter Twelve

A Challenge

Rill sat on the bench, glaring at Uri, and feeling humiliated in front of Jai. He grew sullen, and angry at how Uri treated him.

"Come on, Rill." Jai chided him. "Remember, I know you. You were thinking of getting away alone, weren't you?"

"Well, just in case, I wanted to make sure I knew where the boats were," he lied, trying to keep his real motives to himself. He prided himself at being good at lying. Even though he trusted Jai, he would never let him, or anyone, see the dark thoughts hidden in his heart.

Rill showed the world he was in control. If he could get home and get his mother back on her feet, then he would be in total control of his village. He would be the only one. All the younger children would be gone and in a few years everyone one would look up to him, young and strong. However, if Uri got home too – well, there would be a battle.

Rill realized Jai was talking again.

"I don't want to go home. You understand how my family is."

"Yah," was all Rill said. He saw bruises on Jai many times and knew the method the father used to discipline all his sons.

"If all those beatings my father and brothers gave me haven't hardened me up, nothing will."

"Well," Rill added. "I tried to toughen you up, but you're still a softie."

"My home here is like a mansion. I have my own room. My Dombara father is an elder and an important man, also he is kind to all of us. My older brother and I really hit it off. I'll never go back... to that misery."

"Then you believe all the stuff they've been telling us?"

"Just look at my brothers and you can't deny... we are related."

Rill contemplated the thought he really was born here. He had been introduced to three sisters, older than him. Two were even married with howling brats. Well it didn't make any difference. He would go home, and Jai could stay if he wanted.

"Yah, you fell into a good deal here." Rill's melancholy thoughts changed to fear of what had happened to his mother in his absence, and the old panic arose in him once again. "But my mother hasn't been feeling well lately. I need to get home now, not wait for Uri. He wants to have everything his way."

Jai looking over to where Uri stood watching the children play. "I didn't know Uri back home, but when he stood up to the men at the storytelling, I believe he did it for all of us, not just to make an impression."

Rill sniffed. "Well, he backed down, and I never back down in a fight. He's just a show off." Then his eyes grew dark. "Wait, when that kid came and got him, it was like– like they knew each other. I thought Uri was going to call him by name."

"How could that be?" Jai asked.

Rill squinted toward Uri. "I don't know but I'm sure gonna find out."

He would corner Bibbi the next time he came alone to the play yard. Rill would scare information out of him.

***

Uri divided his attention between Bibbi playing, and Rill and Jai on the bench. Why those two have their heads together? What were they talking about?

He began heading their way, and looking up he saw Kerka and another girl walking down the path. Rill saw them too. Kerka looked so small next to her friend. She was the same age, but shorter. However, her spunky manner gave the illusion of being much larger. She skipped and swung her arms back and forth, all the time talking, and laughing.

Rill stood up and ran toward them. "Where ya goin?" He blocked their way.

"None of your business." Kerka answered, thrusting out her chin.

Rill had his back to Uri, and was unaware of him approaching. Uri smiled.

"You're Kerka and you," Rill leaned forward to look at the girl, "You're Tareen." He stepped back, put his hands on his hips. "If you want to walk in this park, you have to ask me nicely, to let you pass."

Kerka took a step forward. "Rill, you think you have to control everything. Just go away. You're not the boss of this park."

"Oooh, just how I like 'em. Lean and mean." He grabbed Kerka by the wrist and pulled her toward him.

Uri reached them in an instant. "Get your hands off her." He pulled Kerka loose and stood between them. He did not want to start a fight, but that would be up to Rill.

"So that's how it is?" Rill nodded. Then he winked at the other girl, blew Kerka a kiss, and one at Uri also. He turned and went to sit next to Jai.

Uri motioned for the girls to continue, and shot a menacing look at Rill. "Don't ever do that again." He growled, then turned and began to walk down the path glancing toward Bibbi, playing happily, unaware of the situation.

Show off!" He heard Rill yell, getting the last word.

Then Jai laughed, "Oh no, you never back down."

Uri watched Rill turn and shove Jai, almost knocking him off the bench, but Jai just continued to laugh.

Uri knew things were tense between them, once again. He figured Rill would run off, if he got the chance. Uri had to watch him carefully, and think of a way to stop him from pulling any tricks. He knew Rill was ninety-per-cent talk and ten-per-cent action. Still, he couldn't be trusted.

Chapter Thirteen
Questions

Uri ran to catch up to Kerka, "Hey, wait up." He fell in stride with the two girls, eager to learn how they were handling their new lives.

"You didn't keep your promise and look for me." Kerka accused Uri, and pouted.

"I wasn't able to, honest. I'm being watched day and night."

Kerka grabbed hold of his hand. "Take me home. I wanna go home."

"How can I do that? Come on, you know there's no way."

"You're gonna find a way, aren't ya?"

Uri hesitated.

"I know, and you'll go by yourself." She huffed, folding her arms across her chest.

Tareen stood by, nervously shuffling her feet.

"Don't be mad. I want to help you, but I have to get home before I can do that." Uri explained.

"See, I knew you're going home."

"I promise I'll come back for you." Uri wanted to scoop up the little waif, carry her safely home, where he thought she would be happy again. "I really want to help you."

Her face softened and a smile played at the corners of her mouth. "I know ya do, and thanks for helpin' us with Rill."

Uri tousled her hair. Then he noticed it looked good. Smooth, and shiny.

"How are the people you went to live with?" he asked.

"They're very nice. I really like them. It's not so bad staying with them, I guess. We have plenty of food. That's different from home. She pointed in the direction on the far side of the play field, near the forest.

"I live over there, and I have a sister, a little older than you. She brushes my hair and reads to me. And I have a baby brother." She looked at her friend and giggled. "He's so cute. He's learning to walk."

"That's sounds great." Uri smiled.

"My name now is Luwanna. Isn't that pretty?" She lowered her head.

"Yes it is, Luwanna."

Kerka seemed to blush. "I'm glad ya like it."

They both were silent. Then Kerka, now Luwanna, tugged at Tareen. "We gotta to go. We're meeting her two sisters by the swings."

She waved and ran off, leaving Uri wondering why it seemed so easy for her to adjust to the new place they now lived. After all, everyone was here against their will. She wanted to go home, and yet she liked her new family. Confused, Uri shook his head.

When Bibbi caught up with Uri instead of going straight home, he led Uri down a new road.

"That's the school house, over past the trees." Bibbi pointed. "Come this way." He started down the path towards the house.

"Wait Bibbi, let's continue that way." Uri motioned to the right.

"But, that way bypasses the houses and goes to the docks. Why do you want to go down here?"

"No reason," Uri lied.

They had only walked a short distance when Uri saw the docks and the water. There lay the beginning of the Green Sea and the way home.

"Whose boat is that?" he asked pointing to a long, clean looking vessel that sat among many others.

"That belongs to our father, and he must be home by now. Let's go, hurry."

Instead, Uri walked along the dock and studied the boats.

Bibbi was annoyed. "Niliab, please."

"All right, but call me Uri, not Niliab."

They turned and left the docks and water behind, but Uri looked over his shoulder. Many questions ran though his mind. Where could he get a boat like that? Would he be able to sneak one away? Which way on the sea was home?

Uri and Bibbi returned home late in the afternoon. Elajon had been home for a while from his day of fishing and repairing nets. He was washing and joking with the girls, but he looked up as the boys entered the house.

"How was your day, boys?" he asked.

65

Uri grunted and walked past them into the kitchen, looking for something to eat, but Bibbi ran to his dad and told him everything they had done, from the play field to looking over the schoolhouse, to walking down to the docks. Elajon dried his hands and followed Uri into the kitchen.

"Sounds like you were very busy." He paused and affectionately patted Bibbi's cheek. "Niliab, I was wondering, would you like to go out on the boat with me tomorrow?"

Uri straightened, was he really hearing what he thought he was? What an opportunity, and his answer was immediate. "Yes, uh, I mean, I guess so. I haven't got anything else to do."

A broad, crooked smile flashed across Elajon's face. "Good. I thought you might be interested in learning what the fishing business is all about."

Uri felt a dig of guilt. He couldn't care less about fishing, but he grabbed at the chance to learn about sailing a boat and about the sea, so he decided to play along for a while.

Uri spent the rest of the afternoon in the bedroom. His mind continued to plan a getaway. He still didn't want to believe the stolen baby story. However, he noticed a strange coincidence. It was the eye color. Thinking back, he realized all the children had the orange colored eyes. The adult Pinolas had light brown eyes. Here, Dombara adult's eyes shone with a deep, dark amber color. The older the person the darker, and more intense was the color.

He still pondered the mystery as Bibbi poked his head in the doorway. "Come on, we'll be eating soon."

Uri was slow to rise and trudged into the kitchen.

Chapter Fourteen
Creator of All

As Uri entered the kitchen, his mind was still on the questions tumbling around in his brain. Marga removed her apron and smoothed back her hair with her fingertips, a ritual she did every night before worship and dinner. Bibbi, Sarella, and Tika already sat in the living area. He looked at Elajon rubbing his hands together, another ritual. Uri rolled his eyes.

"Well, now let us go into the living area and offer worship to our Creator before we have dinner." The same words, every night.

Uri became increasingly curious about what this worship meant. The family gathered in the large room they called the living area and the father offered up the events of the day and thanked the Creator for His goodness and love. Uri felt it was time to ask questions. Not because he wanted to believe, he had his own beliefs. He knew all about the spirits of his homeland, but he was curious because the family was so intense about this daily event, and Uri wondered if he could poke a few holes into their ideas. He waited until the worship was over and spoke.

Uh, sir, who is this Creator, and where did he come from?"

"Are you asking me to tell you about Him?" Elajon leaned forward.

"Yeh, I guess so."

"Well," he began. "Our Creator always was, is, and always will be. He is all knowing and can be everywhere all the time. He created angels and other spiritual beings, but he desired to create more, because He is the very essence of love. When He began everything, the Universe, and all it contains, He created a planet, far away from ours. It was perfect. There were many different animals, an abundance of fruits, vegetables, and flowers. It was like a wondrous garden, and that is where He placed the first humans. Everything, all of creation, would live forever just as He lives forever. He created them in His image, body, soul, and spirit. It is recorded it took Him six time-periods to complete all of this. His work was finished, and He had his creations with Him eternally.

"One of His angels, in fact, the highest angel, His finest creation, saw all the grandeur of the universe and wanted it for his own. He rebelled and there was a war in Heaven. Now he became an enemy and wanted to destroy all our Creator had done. He went to that planet, and caused doubt to form in the female's mind about the goodness of the Creator. By deceiving them into believing they could be more than they were created to be, they also rebelled, and in that instant all of creation fell into disarray. Sin entered and brought decay and death. Evil began to permeate the entire Universe. It spread into every corner and on every planet"

"Why would a good Creator allow that to happen?" Uri asked.

"He gave His creations the greatest gift of all, free will. Therefore, if he stopped them from rebelling, He would have to take away their free will. He would not force love or obedience from any of the humans, anywhere.

"Ah, but He had a plan. He loved us so much that He yearned to restore the relationship He once had. The Creator sent His Son into the world as a human baby, to live a human life. Only… He would live it perfectly. In doing this, our Creator took on the Evil of the Universe. Sacrificing His only Son, He took the sins of the worlds, burying them and death forever. He defeated The Evil One, thus becoming our Savior. At that instant, just as evil spread throughout the Universe, redemption began and spread. Death died. If we believe in the Savior, we again will have eternal life."

Marga interrupted. "Our supper is getting cold. We can continue this discussion at the table."

They sat around the table, and passed the bowls of food. Uri began to realize there was order in the Dombara family unit. Elajon had the role of provider and spiritual leader. Marga ruled the kitchen and took care of the children. Tika and Bibbi also had their duties. In the Pinola village, the strongest one led the family. This usually was the man or husband, but in some homes, a woman had to take over head of the house. In Beka's case, it was the loss of their parents. However, he knew some women were tough and mean. Uri knew of a few families where there was no leader at all, and chaos abounded.

This system, this family unit the Dombaras followed, felt right to Uri. He respected it.

Reaching for a bowl of vegetables, Elajon asked Uri, "Well, what do you think about what I have told you about the Creator?"

Uri, tried to comprehend what he had heard. "I don't understand. There still is death, sickness, and evil people."

"True." Elajon went on to explain. "But here on Terrasa, the world where we live, it is not like the planet that gave birth to rebellion. Great depravity exits there, terrible cruelty, and horrible diseases. Here we have to deal with only a tolerable amount of decay and death. Everywhere animals grow old and die. Plants also die, and the lights in the sky, they grow old, burn out and die. Everything dies. In addition, animals have babies, new plants shoot up all around us, and new lights are born in the heavens. We also have the ability to create new life. That is why we love our families so very much.

69

"We are created to live forever. What we do with the knowledge of the Savior determines where we spend eternity."

"Here we have peace among people. On that world, they have wars, and unimaginable destruction. People often die when they are young, from diseases and killings."

"Where is this, this so-called planet where all this stuff happened? Which bright light in the sky? Show me."

"I can't, we don't know. Besides, it isn't important. What is important is that it did happen."

Uri studied Bibbi's face for reactions as Elajon spoke. Did he believe this also?

"How do you know this story?" Uri asked Elajon.

"It was told in visions to the prophets in ancient times, and also written in a Great Book."

Uri stared at his plate. "We don't have any knowledge of such a Creator in the tribe I came from. We do have belief in evil spirits, but there is no evidence of a good and loving spirit. Our spirits are evil. They live in caves, and travel on the winds of the deserts." Uri continued.

"Once a year we select a beast of burden from among our animals. The head of each family from the tribe cut themselves, and spread their blood on a leaf that comes from a tree that grows in the desert. Then we pack all those leaves on the back of the animal, and send it into the Land of the Sand, past the farthest well. If the animal does not return, we know the spirits have accepted our offering. But, if the animal comes back, then we have to offer more blood. We do this until the offering is accepted.

"That is how we remove the transgressions we have made through the year. If we are faithful and obedient, the spirits will bring good things, otherwise bad things will fall upon us. Our tribe prides itself on pleasing the spirits."

Elajon shook his head. "No, those superstitions are not necessary. The Creator sent His son, our Savior to be the sacrifice for all. If we confess to our Creator that we are unable to keep His commands, when we accept His Son as our Savior, we never have to worry about transgressions again. He died for all the sins of the Universe, past, present and future. He gives His love unconditionally.

"Everyone in this land believed, but when people left and formed new tribes the old beliefs faded. Unfortunately, something had to replace the void, so stories and superstitions began to form. Mistaken beliefs are part of the evil in the Universe." Elajon looked Uri in the eyes. "My son, the evidence is in the world around you. You can see it in the beauty of the landscape, the wonderful animals that He spoke into existence, a good and loving Creator made it all. And He loves you more than you can ever know."

"I will consider all you have said." Uri answered, but in his heart, he did not believe. "It's a nice story, but it will have to take something extraordinary to happen for me to believe."

"The Creator will provide whatever you need to help you believe." Elajon picked up a piece of meat, put it in his mouth, and smiled.

Chapter Fifteen
The Cousin

Uri poked at his food, forgetting the story he heard. He thought of Rill. What was he planning? How could he maneuver Rill into following the plan Uri had worked on for many anxious days. It would take time to pull it off correctly. Rill didn't have any patience and wanted to leave immediately. He wished he knew Rill better. He needed to figure out how his twisted mind worked. He wanted to talk some sense into Rill, explain the danger of the sea, how acquiring some knowledge of sailing might save their lives. Maybe if he talked to Jai? He had heard Jai had hung around with Rill, ever since they were little.

Elajon intruded into Uri's thoughts. "Your cousin will be visiting us tonight. He is very anxious to meet you. He is the sole witness to the first kidnapping, the one in which you were taken. Maybe he can convince you about the abductions."

"Why would he be able to convince me?"

"When he was eight, he watched the whole episode as it took place, from his bedroom window."

"He is one of our prophets and readers of the Word." Marga added.

Uri smirked. If they thought those things were going to impress him, they were mistaken. He shrugged and continued to push the food around on his plate.

There was a knock on the side door. As it opened, a smiling face greeted the family.

"Come in, come in." Elajon greeted the young man. Bowing his head in respectful greeting, a tall, lean man stepped into the brightly lit kitchen from the back door. He wore no braid. His hair fell over his shoulders in gold curls and he dressed in a pale blue robe. The softest leather sandals Uri had ever seen covered his feet that poked out beneath the robe. The priest stood with both hands behind his back

Marga got up and put another chair at the table. "Would you like something to eat?" She asked.

"No thank you, I just want to meet our new boy, here." He gestured to Uri.

Uri frowned at the plate of food in front of him. He had no interest in meeting anyone, much less a member of this family.

"Niliab... met your cousin Coran." Elajon said.

Coran went over to Uri, smiled stiffly, and extended his hand in greeting. Uri hesitated. He didn't want to endure any more niceties, but his upbringing took over. He pushed his plate away, stood up, and went to meet the grasp. As soon as Uri felt the warmth of a hand, he saw the scar traveling up the young man's arm. Uri knew that scar. The memory had burned into his mind. With a blinding white heat, he flashed back to that night. He saw himself taken from Beka, and saw her shoved to the floor by this very man in robes, standing in front of him. He didn't wear robes that night, but he did wear a mask. Uri pulled back his hand and leapt at Coran, grabbing him by the throat with his left hand, and punching him in the face with his right.

"You killed my sister!" Uri howled repeatedly.

Coran, taken by surprise, fell to the floor, amid flying chairs, and screams emitted by the children. Uri fell on him. The heat of hate shot out from Uri. It emitted from his eyes, his mouth, and the breath from his nose. He allowed it to blind and control him.

In seconds, Elajon and Marga pulled at Uri, and tore him from Coran.

"He pushed her when he was kidnapping me. She hit her head." Uri half yelled and half sobbed as he ineffectively pulled to free himself from their grasp.

Elajon held firmly onto Uri and looked at Coran as he staggered to his feet, wiping the blood from his face with his hands.

"They sent you to his house?" Elajon ask Coran. He seemed to be astonished.

"Yes," Coran replied. "But I didn't know who it would be."

"Those idiots!" the older man exclaimed with fury.

Coran was gasping for breath as he tried to explain. "Niliab, you must understand, I didn't mean to hurt her. She fell."

Blood trickled from Uri's nose. "Don't talk to me, you-you," he fought to think of the worse thing he could call this person. "You evil demon!" He shrugged off the hands that tried to quiet him and ran to his bedroom.

As he lay on the bed, shaken, and his face buried in a pillow, voices filtered in from the kitchen.

"She's not dead, I saw her move. It was simply an accident"

Uri got up and peeked through the crack in the open door. He saw the back of Coran, sitting at the table. Uri fought against the desire to rush at him again.

"It's not your fault, Coran." Marga said as she took a cold cloth from Tika and wiped his face."

74

Uri watched order replacing the turmoil he started. The family picked up the chairs, and arranged them back to the table.

Brushing away the tears from his own face, Uri fell back on the bed, and then rolled over, facing the pillow again. His violent reaction stunned and shocked him. This was the first time he ever attacked anyone. It began and ended before he thought of what he was doing.

He could hear Elajon's voice, shaking and angry. "They were not supposed to match up relatives. Someone made a serious error. Coran, I think it best you go, for now."

"Yes, I agree. I must pray about this, immediately."

Chapter Sixteen
Plans

Uri heard footsteps into his room, and he buried his face deeper in the pillow, trying to push the sight of Beka from his mind. Quiet followed. Then he felt Elajon sit softly on the bed. Several seconds passed before he spoke.

"You must realize Coran did not hurt anyone purposely. Accidents did happen when we came to take all of you back. Our own people were hurt the nights when the Pinolas came to take away our babies. Coran himself was injured the last time. That's how he received the terrible scar on his arm."

Uri was motionless, he felt his stomach constrict, as if to reach up and strangle his heart.

"Coran is a good man." Elajon continued.

Tears flowed into the pillow Uri held close to his face. "I hate him. If I find my sister is dead, I swear, I will kill him."

"But Coran is not capable of hurting anyone. He was the sole witness to the first abduction. It devastated him. He was only eight, Bibbi's age. That incident in his life turned him to look inside for consolation, and that was when he first had visions from our Creator. He began priestly studies, right after that."

Uri turned over, sat up, and glared into Elajon's eyes. "I don't believe in your Creator. I will go back home and continue my life. I will become a great hunter in my land and, if I must, I will come back and hunt down your priestly man like the animal he is."

When Uri saw tears form in the older man's eyes he felt a twinge of sorrow, but immediately hardened his heart against any tender feelings toward any of them. "Go away and leave me alone." He threw himself back down on the pillow, closed his eyes, and in a moment, heard the door softly shut.

He never felt such rage before, in his whole life, and he could not stop trembling. Coran was an enemy and nothing else. He saw the enemy, and attacked. He remembered seeing the terror in Bibbi's eyes as he hid behind Tika, and felt bad about frightening the family, but again hardened his thoughts. He didn't care about any of them. He was going home very soon, and away from this continuing nightmare. However, Uri hoped his behavior hadn't ruined the chances of going out on the water with Elajon in the morning.

He felt a panic welling up. He must learn to sail. Well, he would be very contrite and even apologize if necessary. He would do anything to learn whatever he needed to get home

***

Startled, Uri sat straight up in bed. He must have fallen asleep. He looked out the window, and breathed a sigh. The twin moons hadn't set yet. The last one was just dipping behind the hills, so he still had time to meet with Rill and Jai.

Bibbi was sleeping in the bed across from him, his mouth open and snoring softly. He leaned over and watched him for a few seconds. Walking back to his bed, he slipped on his sandals, deftly moved to the window, and climbed out to the ground below. He left behind the sound of the constant lapping water against the shore. Instead, he listened to the crickets and other night insects buzzing in full volume, as he eased his way along to the play field. The increasing darkness turned the landscape ebony, so Uri kept to the middle of the path. Since he had only been to the play field once, he didn't remember how far it was. In the dark, everything appeared strange and different, and he worried about getting lost. There was an animal barking close by. He hoped it was not wild. Maybe one of those furry things these people kept as pets. He noticed lights far in the distance and wondered where it was coming from. Uri quickened his step.

Arriving at the play field, Uri saw that no one was there, and moved over to the benches. He didn't wait more than seconds when Rill came out from the shadows of the bushes. Uri wondered if he had been there all along.

"Hey, glad you got here." Rill grinned, sticking the tip of his tongue on his lower lip, an irritating expression he often displayed.

"So, been waiting long?" Uri asked, letting Rill know he didn't fool easily.

"I wasn't waiting. I just came through the back way."

Uri let it drop. "Guess what," He was anxious to tell Rill about his chance to go out in the boat with Elajon, and explained it all in detail.

"I'll be able to learn how to maneuver the sails and how to cross the sea. I can find out which way we came from. It's important to find the quickest way across the sea you know, and I have a lot to learn in three days."

"Wow," Rill replied. "What a break."

"Yeh, if he still wants me."

"Why, what do you mean?"

"Well, I kinda had a fight with a so called cousin."

Rill snickered, "Oh yah."

Uri immediately changed his mind about telling Rill the whole story, so he steered the conversation in a different direction. "Anyway, let's go to the docks. We don't have much time." He looked around. "Where's Jai?"

"He said he would try and meet us there."

"What's with him, anyway?" Uri asked as they started down the path.

"I think he's beginning to like his new family. His father is an elder, and they live in a real fancy place in the center of the village. People bring stuff to them, like food and gifts. His brother is only a year older. They get along real good. I think he likes him, a lot. He had trouble with his-" Rill hesitated, "his old family."

"Well, we won't depend on him."

"I guess not."

They continued to walk toward the docks in silence. Uri saw the boats gently rocking in the water. He counted twelve tied up next to each other along the length of the wooden platforms. Then he saw the men, three of them talking together at the end of the furthest dock.

"Are those the guards?" he asked Rill in a low voice.

"Yah," He pulled Uri's arm. "Over here, follow me."

They slid through the trees, down a path to the water's edge, away from the men and the docks.

"See, what I found." Rill pointed through the brush. There a lone boat rested on the sand. Its sail neatly folded, and one fat paddle with a long handle, pointing out from the bow. It was a good size boat, Uri figured sixteen feet in length.

"It's perfect." Rill whispered.

"Okay," Uri rubbed his hands together, "We need to keep our eye on it for a few days. I have to learn how to sail, and I have to learn about the sea. You know, Rill, a storm can come up pretty fast here."

"That's no big deal. Don't be so scared about a few waves."

Uri suppressed the desire to punch Rill in the back of the exposed part of his neck as he peered through the brush. Instead, he grabbed him by the back of his shirt and pulled him, not so gently, away from their vantage point and onto the path leading back to the docks.

"Listen to me Rill. I will meet you in three days at the play field. Be there just after suppertime. Do you understand?"

Rill spat back with sarcasm. "Yah, I guess so. That's not so hard to understand." He obviously didn't like Uri pulling him around.

"We've got to be prepared, and ready to go at a moment's notice if the chance comes up. Can you be ready at a moment's notice?"

"Hm." was Rill's sullen answer.

Uri paused before he spoke again. He looked at Rill's pouting face, defiance written all over it. "We need to be single minded about this if we want it to work. You need me, and I need you." Uri placed his hand on Rill's shoulder to make him feel they were comrades. It must have worked because Rill relaxed and grinned back.

"Sure, I get it Uri. I'll meet you, after supper, three days from now. Learn all you can and I'll find out who that boat belongs to."

"Also, don't say anything to Jai. He might betray us. If he asks, tell him we haven't made any definite plans yet."

They shook hands and went their separate ways, Uri eager to return home before Bibbi woke up. He carefully watched the shadows that played along the edge of the path going home. What Uri didn't see was the small shadow that moved along in the brush ahead of him.

Chapter Seventeen
Deception

Rill watched Uri disappear into the darkness of the night. He almost laughed aloud. What a fool Uri was. Rill realize knowledge of sailing would help, but he would not waste time waiting around while Uri played sailor with his "Father."

He walked over to the boat, unfolded the sail, and hoisted it up the mast. He checked out the tautness, and observed how it worked. He sat in the center, where he thought the best place would be to maneuver the "thing" that directed the sail. He figured he could learn how to do that as he went along. He went to the "rear" of the boat and moved the handle of the rudder, feeling how it worked. Then he lowered the sail and refolded it, leaving everything just as it was, in case the owner of the boat came around during the day.

"Nothin' to it," he boasted. "I can handle this by myself. Just go slow, that's all." Rill felt very clever. He had it all planned. He would leave tomorrow night, weather permitting. First, there was some business to take care of.

He needed to corner that kid, Bibbi. Rill knew he went to the play field everyday and since Uri would be out with his "father" tomorrow, Rill would be able to confront Bibbi without worrying that Uri would be there to defend him. Something wasn't right between those two, and Rill was determined he would find out what it was. He thought Uri was about to call out to Bibbi when he came to get him at the compound. It was something in their eyes, an acknowledgment. Rill felt in his very core of his being...they knew each other.

He suspected there was something to be uncovered. Something he could use against Uri in someway when arriving back home, alone. It would be great to be able to show Uri as a traitor, or even conspiring with the Dombara. Armed with that information Rill believed he would be a hero. A young, smart, and brave man among the tribe of aging fools. He saw himself as their leader. Wonderful. If only he could find out a piece of information, something, anything.

Yes, Bibbi held the answer.

***

Bibbi tracked close behind Uri. He had pretended to be asleep with soft snoring noises. He felt the quiet anticipation coming from the bed across from him and when he heard his older brother get up to crawl out of the window, Bibbi waited for a couple of minutes, and then followed.

He trotted along, keeping to the shadows. Why was Uri going out, in secret?

Was it to meet Rill? Bibbi didn't like Rill. Although he had never talked with him, and only saw him a couple of times, deep down he felt Rill was trouble. Bibbi grew frightened for Uri.

Entering the play field from the side, he stopped. As Bibbi watched from behind the bushes, he could barely see the two figures over at the area of the benches. He noticed Uri stood straighter than Rill, and projected an air of confidence. While Rill tended to slouch down, always moving around nervously.

Bibbi could not get any closer. They would see him, so he stayed where he was. In a few moments, the figures in the dark began to move in his direction. Uri and Rill came back across the field, and walked down the path. Bibbi followed close behind. It was not long before he knew they headed for the docks.

It was hard to keep up. Bibbi had forgotten his sandals, and his bare feet were tender. There were a lot of sharp twigs and rocks. He fell behind, but he knew the general direction and kept on going. When he got to the docks, no one was in sight except for some guards far down at the end. Bibbi crouched low, being very quiet.

"Where would they go?" He thought. *"Now stop and think. Why would they be here?"* It had to have something to do with a boat. Remembering Coran kept his boat in a thicket at the water's edge, he turned, crept through the trees, and stopped in a clump of bushes. From there he could see and hear them.

His brother was not happy with Rill. He knew from the way Uri pulled him up from the crouching position, also Uri's voice gave away his emotions. That anger reminded Bibbi of the evening's events and he shivered. He huddled down closer to the ground, and listened to their plans.

Bibbi suddenly realized they were planning to escape, using Coran's boat. Uri would be going with his father tomorrow and learn to sail. The two would then leave in the boat, and make the dangerous journey back across the Green Sea.

Bibbi's heart pounded as the frightening information seeped across his mind.

He watched as they shook hands, then turned and hurried back, through the bushes, down the path. Bibbi felt a panic rock his soul. What to do?

Soon he was back in bed, shivering with cold and fear. He lay waiting, hardly breathing, and then heard the rustling noises of Uri coming through the window. Even after Uri fell asleep, Bibbi could not quiet down. The events of the last day played over, and over in his mind. How excited he was when Uri asked questions during worship time. At first, he thought this meant his brother was beginning to accept the new

84

situation and the family. After all, Uri had been here almost two weeks. However, when Uri turned on Coran, Bibbi knew different.

The fight between Uri and Coran was so scary, so awful. He did not understand what happened, and why Uri was so angry. That hatred shocked everyone. Perhaps Uri wasn't settling in as he had hoped. Listening to the angry words and the venom he spewed at Coran, he realized his brother must have other plans. Now he knew what those plans were.

Bibbi remembered the day he met Uri. They had been in Pinola Land for a couple of days. Bibbi was so bored and no one was watching, so he began to walk down the valley, away from the caves. Then, he saw the sand. Mountains of it. He had never seen such a sight, and wanted to run right up into it. As he ran, he realized sand was much harder to move about in. It was at that point he saw a figure over the next dune. It was a boy, lying very still. Bibbi watched and continued to narrow the distance between them.

As he got close, the boy stood up and flung a type of weapon at a thing moving in the sand. He missed and went to retrieve the weapon. That was when Bibbi moved up, right behind him. Uri whirled around and Bibbi found himself face to face with a Pinola holding a weapon.

Bibbi tried not to show his fear. They began to talk and he quickly grew to like Uri. Now he knew this was no coincidence, their meeting on the dunes. Bibbi believed it was ordained to happen just that way.

Later, at home, it was with much glee when his father told him to go to the compound and find a boy named Uri. This boy whom he had bonded with so quickly was his brother. At the compound, he saw Uri talking to Rill. When Uri saw him coming, without thinking he almost called out Bibbi's name. Rill's eyes narrowed. What was Rill thinking? Did he realize Bibbi and Uri knew each other? Would he say something to focus suspicion on Uri, and for what purpose? There were many questions in Bibbi's mind, but one thing was for sure. He didn't trust Rill.

Now that he had discovered Uri and Rill's plans, he faced a terrible dilemma. If he told, he was betraying a brother he had grown to love. However, if he didn't tell, Uri would go away forever, and he would probably never see him again. The tears increased and he had to hold back sobs. He could not betray his brother, never. He remembered Uri hadn't told his people he had seen the Dombara patrol, or of the meeting on the dunes. Therefore, Bibbi too, must keep this terrible secret from everyone.

Heavy feelings of responsibility poured into his mind. There were two secrets. The first was their meeting and the second, knowing Uri planned to run away. How could he carry this burden? He was only eight. Bibbi rolled over and placed his cheek on the soft pillow. If necessary, he could be very mature and grown up. Especially if it was important.

Chapter Eighteen
Becoming a Sailor

Uri crept through the window, and slid back in bed after his meeting with Rill. He fell into a light sleep until he heard Elajon moving around in the kitchen. It was still dark. He knew if there was a chance to go out on the boat, he had to humble himself to this older man, his father. Uri dressed and left the bedroom to walk down the short hall. The light from the lantern shone brightly around the kitchen area, and revealed Elajon making his morning hot drink.

"Good morning," Elajon began," would you like some?" He pointed to an extra cup sitting on the counter.

"Yes, please." Uri replied. He thought if he acted just the way Elajon wanted, maybe he would think Uri was repentant about last night's display of anger.

"There are waterproof boots over there for you." Elajon pointed to the doorway.

"It gets very wet in this kind of weather, and those will keep your feet dry."

Uri took the drink and nodded. He tasted the hot liquid and thought. *"Hm, very good, sweet, and strong."*

Marga had baked muffins yesterday, and put them out for the men to eat before they left. Uri had gotten into the habit of using a jelly made from a blue fruit. It was tangy, sweet and grew in the hills just west of them. Tika with her friends went to pick them several times a year. There seemed to be an endless supply of the elliberry.

It wasn't long before they went out the door into the darkness. When they arrived at the docks Elajon motioned for Uri to untie the boat. The knot gave him a problem at first, then he figured it out, and soon they left the shore behind. Uri felt the wet wind on his face. He was nervous at first, but Elajon patiently explained what would be happening.

Elajon showed Uri how to move the boat through the water by switching the sail back and forth. He explained how the rudder worked and let Uri practice. They moved to different areas near the shore, and each time let out the net. Elajon taught Uri how to recognize different fish, and which ones brought the most money. He helped Uri bring in the nets full of fish without losing any. Together, throughout the morning, they filled the boat with several kinds of fish, keeping them all separate and alive so they would be fresh at market.

Uri never worked so hard in his life, but by watching, and listening he learned everything possible. The ability to make a boat go in the direction you wanted was certainly a great skill. He became aware that fishing also took great knowledge and practice. He gained a lot of respect for this older man, was grateful for this opportunity, and quite guilty about the deception. However, he needed to accumulate as much information about sailing as possible in the short amount of time he had, so he played the game.

He saw Elajon occasionally look warily at him, wondering if he was the same boy as last night. Uri realized he must be careful and balance his act. So, just before they were ready to sail into the dock, he returned to his sullen self.

"What's the problem, Niliab?"

"I like sailing, but I think fishing is a lot of hard work. I don't like that."

"Yes, fishing is hard work, but it is a good living. You are almost a man and you will need to learn to do something. It might as well be fishing."

"Yeh, I guess." Was his reply.

***

It was predawn when Bibbi heard his father moving about in the kitchen and watched as Uri rose and left the bedroom, headed to prepare for his first trip out in the boat. He continued to listen to them talk and then he heard them leave. He dozed off. When he opened his eyes, Bibbi saw the black night sky had become a dingy grey. It was cloudy again, and the color of the sky matched how he felt. He hoped it wouldn't rain. It would not be easy for his father and Uri in the boat with bad weather.

It wasn't until he heard his mother and Tika talking that he finally got up, and went into the kitchen. His mother's eyes were very red and he knew she had been crying.

Bibbi, filled with sorrow, thought it would have been better not to bring the children back. It hurt everyone.

After breakfast, Tika brought out the Cussel game. A game with round, small pebbles, and a wooden board.

"Let's play, Bibbi. She offered.

He knew she could have added. "And get our minds off of last night."

"Has Coran been by this morning?" Bibbi asked.

"Yes he was, just after Father and Niliab left. He told Mother he would be staying at the Praying Temple. He will stay in solitude and fasting. He is so upset about the girl he hurt. Shh- Mother is coming."

They focused back to the game in front of them.

89

"I think I will teach Niliab this game tonight, after dinner. It'll be lots of fun." Bibbi said.

"Oh good, maybe we can get a double board and all of us play." Tika added.

Their mother stopped and eyed them, just for a second, then went on with her chores.

After playing games with Tika all morning, Bibbi had lunch, and went to meet his friends at the play field. His mood changed as the grey sky turned blue, and he again felt like his old happy self. He skipped along, but as he arrived he saw Rill, Jai, and Dron on the bench nearest the path. He put his head down and began to walk as fast as he could to pass them.

"Hey, Bibbi," called Rill, "come're."

Bibbi's heart leapt and then seemed to stop altogether. He froze on the path. Rill got up and walked the few paces up to him.

"How come you and Uri got so friendly so fast, huh?"

"I don't know what you mean." Bibbi said.

"You knew each other before, right?"

Bibbi felt terrified of this bully. "No, of course not."

"I think you did. I know Uri's never been here before, but maybe you've been in our land."

Bibbi watched Rill's eyes narrow and felt he was looking into true hatred. A cold fear spread across Bibbi's chest. How could such things be? He realized that these boys were from a different land, a different way of life. He had no experience in dealing with these differences, and Bibbi knew the helplessness he felt showed on his face

"No." Bibbi tried to get around Rill. "I don't know what you're talking about." He pleaded, "Please let me pass." holding back the tears.

"Hey, Rill, let the kid go." shouted Dron.

Rill straightened and the smoldering emotion in his eyes dissipated.

"Please, oh please." Bibbi thought.

Rill bent down so he could whisper in Bibbi's ear. "I know you were there."

The blood drained from Bibbi's face. He swallowed hard and ran around Rill. As he ran, he looked over his shoulder at the three boys and saw Rill doubled up with laughter, a hard, course laughter. Bibbi turned, and quickly joined his friends at the Cho field.

Chapter Nineteen
Confrontation

During the afternoon when Bibbi took a break from the game, he looked over at the three boys. He was to far away to hear, but Jai asked Rill something that caused him to react violently. Bibbi stopped cold and watched a rampage of rage. Screaming at both Jai and Dron, his mouth form the words *hate* and *kill*. What kind of people were they, these boys from the land of the Pinolas that would hate and harbor the desire to kill? The intense fear he felt turned to pity. Bibbi tried, but couldn't comprehend it all. Rill must have lived with violence and ugliness.

It was time for Bibbi to leave the park and head down the path to his home. Father and Uri would be home soon, or maybe they were already, but Rill was still at the bench Bibbi had to pass. If he ran as fast as he could, maybe he would get by Rill.

He took off running, but just as he reached the boys, Rill stepped out in Bibbi's path.

"*Okay.*" Thought Bibbi. "*I'm ready for him, I think*".

"Hey, slow down, little guy." Rill reached for him. "We aren't done yet."

"Oh yes we are. I've got nothing to say to you." Bibbi avoided Rill's grasp at first, but Rill, bigger and faster, caught up to him.

"You leave me alone. Uri wouldn't like you hassling me."

"What? Are you going home to tattle and get your big brother to beat me up?"

Bibbi looked straight at Rill, "Why is everything so violent with you?" he asked flatly.

"Huh," The question surprised Rill, and with that hesitation Bibbi was off and running down the path.

"We aren't done, you little creep." Rill yelled after him.

Bibbi didn't look back.

***

Elajon and Uri returned and tied the boat up, but there was still work to do. They pulled out the day's catch, and filled up the fishmongers waiting baskets. Then as Elajon talked business, Uri waited, still on the boat. He went over everything again, in his mind. The way to tack, or move direction. How to turn the boat, how to control the rudder, how to approach large waves, and much more. He burned them into his mind.

"I have to go with him a few more times before I'm sure I know what I'm doing." He thought. *"That should be all I need, just to get across the sea."*

Elajon motioned to Uri. It was time to head for home. The markets were opening soon and the people from the village would come to get their next few days supplies.

They did it different here than back home. In the Pinola village, the markets opened early and closed when the fruits and vegetables ran out. Here, the markets opened in the early afternoon, because the fishermen arrived with their catch after the sun reached high in the sky. Then people were able to buy fish, fresh from the sea.

Uri followed Elajon the short distance to the marketplace. Stalls, constructed from large poles and thatched roofs, had an air of permanence. In fact, the whole market place seemed to have been in the same area for a long, long, time. People milled about, shopping, talking, and some sat at provided seating areas as they drank a dark liquid.

Uri noticed with clarity, the difference in the Pinola and Dombara societies. Here people ate many fish, along with the Ovi's they occasionally killed, and ate their eggs. Back home fruits and vegetables were the mainstay, and a meal of meat was a great treat. Uri knew his people desperately needed more meat in their diet. Why didn't they catch fish? Uri puzzled. Then it came to him, they never thought of going to the sea and learn to fish, perhaps because the sea was at least an hour from their village. What a revelation. He could show the men of the village how to fish and help his people with this great knowledge. His face showed the glee he felt, and he enjoyed Elajon watching him as they walked swiftly home.

Uri thought, *"He's probably trying to figure me out. That's okay. Let him try. He will never understand or know anything about me."* This made him feel satisfied and his step was lighter than before.

When they got home, he looked around for Bibbi, and finally asked where he was.

"He went to the play yard earlier." Marga answered, then turned and as she removed her apron and reached for a sweater, she asked, "Would you please take Sarella and meet Bibbi there? Father and I need a couple hours to do some shopping and Tika is not here. It's so hard to take the little one along." She opened the door and called over her shoulder. "Thank you."

They were gone before Uri could respond. Oh well, just another thing to endure for another day.

Uri followed down the path to the park and play field. He reluctantly allowed Sarella, to hold his hand as they walked.

She chattered on and on, but Uri didn't hear a word she said. In his mind he was busy, practicing handling the sail.

They were almost at the play field when Bibbi came towards them, walking very fast. His head was down and Uri noticed how pale he looked.

"Hey, Bibbi, slow down." Uri said.

Bibbi walked past. "I'm going home." He muttered.

"No you can't. I'm supposed to take Sarella to the play field, so you have to go back."

"I don't want to. I'm hungry and I want to go home."

Uri then put his arm around Bibbi and said, "I'll take you over to the town later, and we'll get something to eat there."

Tears began to form in Bibbi's eyes. "I don't want to go back."

"Tell me what happened. Why are you afraid?"

"Rill was there and he- -well he..." Bibbi didn't finish his sentence.

"He what?" Uri now began to feel agitated with Rill.

"He hassled me."

"About what?"

"Just, stuff." Bibbi sighed and turned around. "I just don't want you to say anything to him, please."

"Don't worry; he won't come near you now that I'm here. We'll ignore him and walk through the play field to the other side by the swings. What did he say to you?"

"Just mean things." Bibbi said, looking at the ground.

"Like what?"

"I don't want to talk about it. He's mean and full of hate."

"Did he ask you things about me?" Uri persisted.

'I don't want to talk about it! I don't want to go back to the play field. I just want to go home!"

Uri couldn't tear any more information from Bibbi. What did Rill say to upset him so? It had to be something very important. What could Rill be up to, and what could he possibly want from his eight-year-old brother?

Chapter Twenty
A Walk Through Town

The second day Uri went out with Elajon they returned later in the afternoon. They didn't even throw the nets in the water for fish today, instead Elajon showed Uri the finer points of sailing. They sailed around the jetties and coves by the west side of the land and then, taking their time, went back to the docks.

Once again, when he got home and cleaned up, Marga asked him to take

Sarella and Bibbi for a walk. Reluctantly he agreed... he had no choice.

With Bibbi on one side and Sarella on the other, they walked the short distance to the village. Uri wanted to find Jai, and talk to him about Rill. It didn't matter if the children with him or not. Uri would think of something to distract them. Jai was the link between Rill and everything else. Jai knew how Rill's twisted mind worked.

Uri slowed his steps as they came to the outskirts of the village. "Bibbi, do you know how to get to Jai's home? Do you know which elder is his father?"

"I think it is Elder Ando. That family lives right in the center of the village. He has a big stone house with wide steps going up to the front door."

"He must be a very important man." Uri commented.

"Yes, he leads the 'Days of Reading' and is next in line to be the village chief."

"What are 'Days of Reading'?"

Bibbi looked up. His eyes squeezed closed and his face took on an intense, grown-up expression. "Those are seven days scattered throughout the year that the whole village goes to the Temple of Prayer, and Elder Ando reads from the Sacred Book. Those are very holy days."

"Hmm..." was Uri's answer. "Come on, show me the way to this fancy house."

The village streets were very narrow and winding. Soon Uri wasn't sure which way they came from. Homes were closely spaced on each side of the streets and as they walked along, they got bigger and higher. Down the side streets were vendors in permanent patio-like structures. They looked as though they had seen many years at their locations. Uri could smell cooking fish, steaming vegetable soup, and occasionally a faint odor of leather and fresh cut wood, drifting up from those bypasses. There were voices calling out to people as they passed by. Trying to encourage them to stop and see what magnificent goods they sold. The streets were noisy but not loud, busy but not chaotic. People passed them on the left as though that was an unsaid rule, and a few led strange looking animals by a tether. They had short grey hair and long narrow ears. Packs lay across their backs bulging with goods.

"What are those animals?' Uri whispered.

"Those are Noogans."

Uri noticed they were larger than the Kavacs, those small, furry, hoofed beasts with little horns that people kept for their rich milk.

Most of the women had their heads covered with a striped cloth, while the men wore a small, dark cap under which the

Dombara braid hung down their back, decorated with beads. Many wore the beaded jackets. He didn't see any women alone, only in groups, and they wore a lot of jewelry. Colorful beads and polished stones strung together with cords. Uri thought how nice it would be if he could get some jewelry for Beka.

Uri noticed a group of young men standing around one of the market stalls. They were dressed differently, their haircut very short, and their manor seemed hostile. "Who are those men? They aren't Dombaras."

"No, they are Bast people. I don't like them."

"Why?" Uri asked.

"Everyone says they keep secret medicines and poisons. No one knows where they get them. When the Bast people come to sell their things at the marketplace, they price everything very high."

"How do they get away with charging so much?" Uri asked.

"Their goods are special. Like the furniture. No one else can make furniture with the materials the Bast use, because the Tangleroot trees only grow in their area. It is a hard, shiny wood, and everyone wants to have a chair or table made from it. A lot of strange things grow only near their village."

"Why can't the Dombaras go there and harvest those things."

"It's said the Bast would kill anyone going near their territories. Kill them with the poisons they have."

Bibbi grabbed Uri's hand and led him down a wider street. "Here, this way."

At the end of the street stood a large, stately stone structure. Uri was amazed at the intricately carved stones and wide stairs that led up to the shiny wooden door.

"Oh, this is where Cherka lives." Sarella pulled on Uri's hand. "She's my best'est friend." Then she ran up and turned a handle on the side of the door.

The door swung open and there stood Jai. Next to him was a taller boy, a little older, and Uri noticed they could have been twins. Both had the same fair completion, long lanky body, and wide inquisitive eyes. As he studied the two boys, a tiny girl ran between them, squealing at the sight of Sarella. The two little girls ran into the dark abyss of the house and disappeared.

Chapter Twenty-One
A Talk With Jai

Uri was amazed by the close resemblance of Jai and the other boy, even the little girl looked just like them. There was no way he could argue that Jai was not from this family. His doubts grew. Maybe the Dombaras were telling the truth.

"That's alright," Bibbi explained, mistaking the dumbfounded look on Uri's face for concern about Sarella. "She'll be back out in a few minutes."

Uri couldn't care less about Sarella. He ran up to greet Jai, suspiciously glancing at the older boy. "How are things going?" Uri greeted him.

"Good to see you, uh- this is Goth, my brother. This is Uri - from- from-" he stuttered.

"Hello." The young man extended his hand in greeting and Uri gave a quick and hasty response.

"Uh, Jai, can I talk to you for a minute?" Uri asked.

"Sure." He looked back at Goth. "Hey, take Bibbi in to see Frash."

Bibbi smiled. "Yah, I know Frash. He's in my class at school." They disappeared into the same darkness.

Jai walked down the steps with Uri. "What's up?" he asked as they reached the bottom.

"Are you happy here?" Uri began. "You sure live in a big house, and with an important family."

"I guess the house is a lot bigger than we are used to, but the family is wonderful. I don't think you knew my Pinola family, but things were not good. I would have run away a long time ago, if there had been anywhere to run. Here they love me and treat me with honor. I belong here, with them."

Uri was confused. "That's great, but don't you miss your family back home?"

"Not my father." He grimaced. "Maybe my mother, a little, and my only sister, but not my older brothers. They're as mean as my father."

"I don't remember seeing you at school. I don't think I know who your Pinola father is."

"You can't miss him. He has a red mark on his face."

Uri thought and shook his head.

"Well," Jai explained. "You know the school back home consisted of the three tribes, so my father didn't want us to go. He's suspicious of the other tribes."

"I didn't go much either." Uri admitted. "I can read and write, and I can add and subtract... that stuff. I'd rather be out on the dunes, hunting."

"We couldn't do anything like that. We had to stay home and work. He grew crops, and raised a few Kavacs."

"It sounds like you really had a hard go." Uri responded. He could not comprehend why people were so mean to their own kind, the people they should love and take care of.

"Goth tells me the school here is really great." Jai said. "We learn about a lot of different things, not just reading and writing. I am very happy. I wish you could be happy here too."

"Nope, you know I'm going back with Rill, but- what's the matter with him? I can't figure him out."

"Watch your back. Rill has to have his own way." Jai sat down on the step. Uri followed suite.

"I've known Rill since we were little." Jai continued. "His father and my father were friends. His father beat him all the time, more than mine beat me. Then, when Rill was about five, his father died. I'm not sure from what, but he had already done a lot of damage to Rill. That left Rill and his mother alone. I remember," Jai's voice became quiet, and he looked up, at the sky above. "She was sickly then and never got better. Rill cared for her all alone, but he was embarrassed of her and of being poor. It seemed he always needed or wanted to be better than everybody." Jai looked at Uri, 'I think that's why he pushes people around, but he never did that to me. I guess he needed one friend."

"What was he doing to Bibbi yesterday?" Uri asked.

"I'm not sure. He seemed to think – well - he was suspicious of something. I don't know what."

"Did you hear what he said to him?"

"No, I couldn't hear. He talked low, like - right at Bibbi."

Uri paused and stared ahead. "I guess you won't be leaving with us, but please, don't give us away."

"Oh no, you can count on me. I won't say anything to anyone. I really don't know anything anyway. Just be careful of Rill, he can be treacherous."

They sat silently for a while.

Uri took a deep breath. "Do you believe the story of the stolen babies?"

"Absolutely, in fact I think when you get back you should try to find out why, and what happened. Why did the tribe steal babies? Maybe that's a good reason to go back. I believe in the Creator and the Savior. My family has told me all about the story of creation and the fall. How evil got into the Universe. Have you heard?"

Uri stared at Jai. "You believe all that? Those are just stories."

"I don't think so. There has to be something good that created all this."

"Well, maybe so. I don't know."

"Promise me you will think about it anyway. If you find out why that terrible thing happened, you know, with the babies and all. If you find the truth, try to let me know. The truth is very important."

"That I agree with. Truth is the most important thing. Thanks. By the way, what's your name here?"

"They let me keep my name, Jai. Isn't that great?'

"Yeh, I am happy for you. I wish we had been friends back home."

Jai looked hard at Uri. "So do I."

Chapter Twenty-Two
The Attack

A horrible, clanging noise penetrated deep into Uri's bones. He covered his ears with his hands and looked up from his dinner plate, across the table at Elajon.

"The alarm!" Elajon cried.

"W-W-What…" Uri stuttered as the deafening noise became louder.

Elajon motioned to Uri. "It's the village alarm. Follow me. There has been an accident, and we must go."

Uri hesitated. They had only been home an hour or so from the walk into town.

"I'm on the committee, I must go. Come with me, please." Elajon's voice carried an urgency that motivated Uri to move.

Finding his feet he joined Elajon, and together they ran, meeting up with others spilling out onto the pathway. They ran down past the docks, past the community facilities. More joined in as they ran passed the seashore, and up to the cluster of homes on the other side of the village. Uri found it hard to keep up with Elajon. He had to admit, the older man was strong and in good shape. As they arrived, Uri notice all the people crowded around one of the homes. A man came up to Elajon and began to explain what had happened.

"It was an attack on a girl, one of those that were brought back." He began. "She wandered into the forest with some friends and..."

"Terrible, terrible." A woman interrupted him. "She is in bad shape. The healer and one of the priests are with her now.

Uri's heart leapt into his throat. This was the very area Kerka had pointed to when she explained to Uri where her home was located. "What girl, what is her name?" He demanded.

They looked at him, hesitating.

"What is her name? Tell me!"

"I think she is called, Luwanna." The woman said.

Uri shoved everyone aside, struggling through the crowd of people clustered around the door. He entered the house, dark and heavy with silence. He barely noticed the small family huddled tightly together in a corner. The man from that group stepped out and touched Uri's arm.

"Please, are you Uri?" He whispered.

"Yes"

"Luwanna talks about you all the time. If she sees you, it might help her fight for her life."

Uri felt the hair on the back of his neck stand up. Her life, it was that critical. He nodded at the man, and went to the doorway of the bedroom. There on the bed lay a small figure. Her hair matted with blood, and her face deathly pale. She lay very still. Her left arm, heavily bandaged, oozed blood onto the bed.

Uri stared at her small, frail, wounded body, and then pushed past the healer to the side of her bed. He fell on his knees, and a great sob escaped from him. "Is she dead?" he asked, his eyes never leaving her.

106

"No, she is badly hurt, but she will survive." He knew that voice. It was Coran.

Then the healer spoke. "But she has lost the use of her left arm. The animal badly mangled it."

Tears fell from his eyes over his face. "What did this to her?"

"It was a Getiru."

"What is that?" Uri looked up at the healer.

"A large forest cat. They seldom come this close to the village. It seemed to be a young one that was looking for food."

Uri dropped his head on the bed.

"She was very lucky." Coran explained. "Someone heard screams from the children and rushed over. It was killed immediately."

Luwanna moved her right hand, and touched Uri's hair as it spilled onto the bed.

"Uri, are ya there?"

He lifted up and looked at her. "Yes, I'm here." In anguish, he knew he had failed to protect her, and his heart broke as she tried to smile at him.

"Don't cry, I'm okay."

Anger replaced the grief and he rose, looking to the healer, avoiding Coran's intense gaze.

"Where is this Getiru? I want to see it." He didn't know why this urge to look upon the cause of Luwanna's torment overwhelmed him, but it filled every fiber of his being.

The healer stared at him, and then agreed. "Come, follow me."

They wrestled though the crowd out to a clearing in the forest. Several men stood around, softly talking, and looked over at the two as they approached. Without speaking, everyone parted and exposed the body of the Getiru, lying on the ground. The back of its head smashed on one side. The sight of the death mask produced a shudder that coursed though Uri's body. The lips pulled back in a frozen, open mouth howl. Dried blood matted the mottled, yellow striped fur from the head down to the front paws. The face of the Getiru appeared wide and bony and a crude representation of ears perched on either side of its dome-shaped head. Uri thought it looked deformed or a mutated beast of a sort.

He wished it were alive so he could kill it himself.

"Beason killed it." The younger man spoke. "He was carrying an axe at the time, heard the girls scream, and was close enough to reach them in time."

Sour gall rose in Uri's throat. He turned away from the animal, ungainly hideous in death, and stumbled back down the path to the cluster of homes. As he returned to the front of the house, he saw Jai, and moved toward him. Anger shot from Uri's eyes.

"So, this is what your great and loving Creator is like." Uri spat the words out through his teeth. "He allows innocent children to be mangled and maybe even die. Kerka is laying in there a bloody mess." Using her Pinola name purposely, he glared at Jai.

"The Creator didn't do this. We live in a fallen Universe. Accidents happen all the time. You know that."

Uri shrugged off Jai and ran back into the house. Coran, the healer, and the parents of Luwanna stood inside her room. Uri moved close to Coran's face.

"This is what the Spirit you pray to and worship does? He allows this kind of pain and horror to happen." Uri waited to see what Coran would say.

"Please understand. We do not know why things like this happen. The Creator will use all things for good. He can see from the beginning to the end of time. We only see a tiny bit..."

"No, this can not be for any good. A girl has been crippled for life."

"How do we know what good will come from this? We don't know The Creator's plan for her life."

The healer spoke to Uri. "Pray, my son. Pray He will show you His way. Have faith."

Uri curled his lip back over his teeth. "Pray to what? Have faith? Never. At least our people know the things that the evil spirits can do. We know and can avoid much of it." He turned and knelt again at Luwanna's bedside. He saw Coran hold back the healer from continuing.

Uri put his lips close to Luwanna's right ear. "I'm not leaving until you are well."

She turned her eyes at him and whispered. "No Uri, follow your plans. Don't change things. I'll be fine. Don't blame The Creator for this. It was our stupidness for going to the forest."

Uri gasped, could she be falling under the spell of this religion also?

He contained himself and continued. "How can I go away with you like this?"

"It's important. You gotta leave as planned." She whispered into his ear. "I believe The Creator has plans for you."

He bowed his head. He knew she was right about leaving. It must be done quickly, or not at all. Rill would not wait, and if he left without him, Uri knew there would never be an opportunity to get away again.

Uri sank to the floor. He would stay through the night to convince himself she would survive. "Sleep Luwanna. I am here. Nothing will hurt you now. Sleep."

The fragile child smiled and closed her eyes. There was a look of comfort on her face, and Uri knew it was because of his presence.

Chapter Twenty-Three
A Hard Lesson

Rill slipped out the door of the house where he had been living with the two "old uglies", as he loved to call them. He overheard there had been some kind of an accident, and everyone rushed to see what had happened. Taking advantage of the commotion in the village, Rill hurried away, down to a thick area of brush he found days ago. He sat lingering, nestled up against a bush until all was deserted, and darkness descended. His mind wandered as he waited. Angry thoughts meandered to those "old uglies" who tried to convince him they were his parents. At first, they left him alone, but as the days passed, the old man began to question him. Then they both tried to give him orders. That was not going to happen, not to Rill. Nobody ever told him what to do or how to behave.

When it was finally dark, he emerged from the covering, turned and headed into the heart of the town. Days ago, on a back street, he found a place that young people gathered, some from other tribes. It was the only place he could get liquor. The liquid was harsh and tasted bad, but it dulled the pain in his head. This malady had bothered him off and on for many months, but since he arrived, it increased in frequency and intensity.

Rill opened the door to a dilapidated wooden building that stood amid others on a back street, and entered a dark, smelly room. The odor of smoke, cheap drink, and sweat hung over everything like a damp towel. He maneuvered through the crowd, many from the Bast tribe. This was one of the few places they frequented outside of their own village. Many talked in a different dialect he didn't recognize, and they watched him suspiciously, as he pushed his way through to a table against the back wall. Standing over two young men seated at the table, he threw down some money.

"I want a drink."

"Hey Rill, who'd ya get that wad a' money from?" One of them asked.

"Let's just say they don't need it as much as me." He sat down as one of the men gave him a tall bottle. Rill poured the dark colored liquid into a cloudy glass that was next to him and downed it in one gulp. It burned as it went down, but then numbed everything.

Rill looked into their heavy lidded eyes. "Don't get any funny ideas, boys. I have equipment to protect what belongs to me." Rill winked at them and poured another.

He didn't stay long, just to rid his head of the pain, then he left the town behind, and ran along the path to the water's edge. He smiled to himself, his mind a little fuzzy from the drink, but he felt great. Now was the moment he had carefully planned. He was leaving this all behind, the green land, the rain, those old people, and Uri.

The boat still rested on the bank. No one had moved it. Well, now the boat was his. He looked up into the black sky speckled with stars. A soft breeze rustled through the trees. Good, it would help move things along.

He pushed the boat into the water, jumped in, and raised the triangular sail.

"*See,*" Rill said to himself, "*that was easy.*" Then he realized that funny looking paddle was still on the bank. He held on to the towrope with one hand, and jumped in the ankle-deep waves, struggling back to shore. Grunting, he maneuvered into the boat the heavy piece of wood that someone had tried to carve into a paddle.

The breeze began to pick up as he pushed the boat out to sea, but the wind blew directly from the water onto the land. Taking every bit of strength he had, Rill pushed from behind, only to gain a few feet. All of a sudden, the wind changed, and to his surprise, the boat began to edge away from him. He grabbed the side and hoisted his upper body over the edge, and tumbled in.

Lying on the floor of the boat like a big fish, Rill rolled over and grabbed the rudder. It was sluggish in his inexperienced hand and the boat floundered, bobbing back and forth. He grabbed the rigging that guided the sail, but Rill didn't have the slightest idea what to do next. A gust of wind tore it from his hand, and he watched as the sail went flying from one side of the boat, over to the other. He tried to duck as it flung around, but he wasn't quick enough. As it hit him, blinding pain ripped though his head.

Rill's heart pounded with fear as he realized he had no control. However if the sail was down, he could paddle back to the shore. He held the back of his head, crawled to the mast, and as he lowered the sail, another gust hit the falling cloth. The boat wobbled and pitched sideways, throwing Rill overboard. Blood dripped into the water from a scrape on his arm. The cold water reviving him for the moment, he looked for the towrope in the dark water. Splashing and flailing around, he managed to get hold of it, and painfully dragged the boat onto the sandy beach. By this time, he was exhausted and beat up. He fell on the wet sand, and let the coolness extinguish the fire in his head while darkness filled his mind.

Rill suddenly woke, unaware several hours had past. He felt groggy and nauseous. Gathering all the strength he had, he got to his knees. The realization he would have to do it Uri's way infuriated him.

Rage replaced the pain, and lifting both fists in the air, he cursed the darkness. He cursed the wind, he cursed the

Dombaras for bringing him here, and finally he cursed Uri, because he knew Uri was right. He wasn't going home tonight. Rill loathed admitting it, but managing a boat did take skill. Skill he did not have.

Chapter Twenty-Four
Last Days

"Oh no Niliab, don't" cried Bibbi. "Don't, please not again." He looked into Uri's eyes, desperately pleading with his brother. Uri stared back, his face grim and rigid. Then a cruel smile grew wider. Bibbi grabbed Uri's arm, but ignoring him, Uri pulled away and swiftly removed Bibbi's last pebble from the Cussel board.

"Ah-ha-ha." Uri laughed.

He could see by the disgusted look, Bibbi did not think it was funny.

"I teach you to play this game, and you go and beat me four times in a row. I'm not playing with you again." Bibbi pouted and grabbed at the colored pebbles, putting them back in the pouch.

"Oh, don't be like that."

Bibbi turned away, and stomped into the kitchen just as his father entered the house.

"What are you upset about?" Elajon asked.

"He's mad because I beat him at Cussel." Uri explained.

Elajon grabbed Bibbi by his shoulders. "That is not the way to behave. When we play, it's for fun. Anger disturbs your spirit, and you lose your peace."

Bibbi looked at the floor.

"Anger only leads to evil, and takes our focus off the Creator. Do you feel love for Niliab when you are angry with him?"

Tears welded up in Bibbi's golden eyes. "No father, I'm sorry Niliab"

Uri stammered. He had goaded him into that anger. "Oh forget it Bibbi. I was just teasing you, teasing about losing." He ruffled Bibbi's hair. "I'm sorry too."

"Good," said Elajon. "A lesson learned."

Elajon hadn't taken him out that morning and Uri wondered if it was because the attack on Luwanna. Elajon knew it had deeply disturbed him. On the other hand, maybe he did or said something to make Elajon suspicious. Maybe it was because today the wind blew unusually strong, and Elajon was being protective.

Whatever the reason, he wasn't about to ask. Uri was very worried about Luwanna's condition, and hope to get away to see her once more before he left. Right now, he enjoyed staying in the house and spending time with Bibbi. Uri realized he was really going to miss him.

While they were in worship, Uri surprised himself by asking more questions about the stories of the Creator, and of the Savior he had heard over the last several days. He purposely avoided bringing up the unjust allowances of pain and suffering, mainly because he had heard all the excuses and couldn't bear the repetition. He stuck to the obvious.

"How do you know these stories are correct? Maybe over the years things got changed and were added."

"It had been written in a book, The Sacred Book. In the past, long ago, before the tribes broke away, several prophets had visions and visitations. They wrote them all down in a

116

book. Seven times during the year the Elders read from that book." Elajon explained.

"Oh, Bibbi told me about that." Uri nodded.

"The stories have not changed. The facts are the same today, just as they were then. Our Creator does not change. He is the same yesterday, today, and forever. That is why we can totally trust in Him."

Again, Uri felt a stirring inside, but shut it out. Nothing he heard had made sense, and he did not see any loving or kind acts by this Creator. He thought of Luwanna, crushed and hurt. Even if deep down he wished Elajon could explain all his doubts away, Uri knew he was not about to give him an opportunity to do that.

When dinner was finished, he announced he was going out to meet with some of his friends. The parents looked concerned, but said nothing as Uri walked out the door. He knew they were worried when out of their sight, but they wouldn't stop him.

Well, so be it. Tonight was his meeting with Rill and nothing could prevent it.

The night again felt cool and damp. There seemed to be a promise of rain, but the wind died down as the sky grew dark. Uri reached the play field and waited alone at the benches. Soon the bushes parted and Rill emerged.

Uri was immediately irritated. "Hey, can't you use the path like everyone else."

"Oh, don't start with me. It's been a bad day."

"Why, what happened now?"

Rill was jumpy. He looked up and down, back and forth. "The old uglies are getting tough with me. They can't control everything I do and they don't like it. I won't cooperate with them. They don't know what to do about it, and send me to my

117

room." He laughed. "So I crawl out the window." Rill looked up at the sky. "I wanna get outa here." It was more of a plea than a statement.

"Well, that's what I'm preparing for. " Uri said. "But I think we should wait a couple of nights for some moonlight to help us see what we're doing and where we're going." Uri noticed the scrapes on Rill's arm. "Say, what did you do to yourself?"

Rill looked away and changed the subject. "I found out that the boat belongs to some guy who isn't even around right now. I hear he's off in some temple somewhere. We better leave before he comes back 'cause there's nothin' keepin' us here."

"You have a point." Uri agreed, although he didn't want to. He wanted to see Luwanna once more, but he felt something else. Could it be fear? He pushed the emotion aside and replied, confidently, "I'm pretty sure I can sail that boat just fine. Yes, I can do it."

"Good, I was beginning to worry. I'll meet you at the boat tomorrow night, just as the High Hour approaches." Rill stepped closer to Uri. "Be there or I'll go alone."

"Rill, you don't know what to do with that boat." Uri warned.

"I don't care."

Uri saw a flash of hesitation cross Rill's face. "You'd better care. By the way, bring fresh water with you. We can't drink the sea water." Uri added.

"I'll be prepared." Rill disappeared into the darkness of the bushes.

Chapter Twenty-Five
A Father's Plea

Uri stood looking for a long time at the place where his adversary, plus co-conspirator, disappeared. Then he started down the path to the docks. He decided, if they were leaving the next night, he had better check the boat to make sure all the equipment was ready for sailing. He crept over to the shoreline where the boat sat alone. He noticed the water was lower than the time before. It must have something to do with the tides Elajon had tried to explain. Uri didn't understand what tides where. All he understood was they went up and down, and it changed the shoreline.

He hoped the water wasn't down this far tomorrow night. It was a long way to the water's edge and would be difficult to push the boat that far. He checked the sail and saw that one large, flat paddle was on the bottom of the boat.

Then he noticed water in the bottom. Uri grew suspicious. *"I thought Rill said no one had touched it. Where did the water come from? It wasn't there before."* He thought. Doubt and worry entered his mind. Well, he never could believe anything Rill said.

There were ropes coiled up on the opposite side of the place were the paddle laid. Everything seemed to be in order and Uri felt relieved. They should be able to get across the sea in a little over an hour. That seemed about how long it took to get here. Soon he would be in his own bed.

Uri smiled and headed back to the house. As he approached, he noticed a faint light in the living area. He had only been gone for a few hours. That length of time shouldn't cause any suspicion. Someone must still be up. Usually everyone was in bed by this time of the night.

He was careful to monitor his words and actions in front of Elajon and Marga, so no one would think he had thoughts of leaving. He was pleased with himself and thought what a surprise it would be when they found him missing. Satisfied with his cleverness, he boldly opened the front door and walked inside the house. Elajon was in his chair, waiting. He sat by a small light, his arms crossed over his chest. Uri stopped as he looked at the older man with surprise.

"Niliab, can we have a talk?"

"Uh, sure." Uri sat in the chair opposite Elajon, and felt his heart begin to pound. *Here we go.* He searched his mind to see if there was anything, anything at all, he could remember he said, revealing the events planned for the next day.

Elajon was quiet for a long moment. He looked up at Uri and sighed.

"I know you aren't happy here. We tried to make you feel at home. Is there anything that would help? Would you rather we use your other name? Can you tell us what we can do to make you happy?"

"Yeh, take me home." Immediately Uri was sorry he said that.

Elajon hung his head and rubbed his hands together. "I'm very aware of that desire. Also, I am not totally ignorant of the fact you are planning to escape, and sail across the sea."

Uri didn't reply. To many lies had already been told and he knew denial was foolish.

"I would strongly advise against that. You don't have the skills to safely manage a voyage that far. The sea is very

120

treacherous, and many things can go wrong. You need much more experience."

Uri remained silent.

Elajon waited, and then spoke again. "I'm sure you have noticed we have a thriving society here. There are many more opportunities for you to have a happy, successful life with us, in this village. The Pinola tribe struggle just to exist, because of the terrain, the lack of water, and partly because of their stubbornness."

Elajon stood up and walked across the room, looking out the window. "Many years ago there were efforts to introduce animals, like the Ovi's and every time, we were rebuffed. We offered to trade goods, but they denied our efforts. The Pinolas are very superstitious. As long as they believe in evil spirits and continue with their superstitions, they will struggle."

"I never felt like we were struggling. I had a good life there." Uri said in defensive, but he admitted to himself, Elajon had an interesting point. He often thought the elders used those beliefs to keep a strong hold on the people and their lives. Uri also knew the Pinola's would benefit by raising Ovi's and using the eggs for food. Trading the wona meat for fish would enhance their tedious diet. He liked the taste of the fish and already thought of fishing when he got home.

Elajon began again. "When we found that it was the Pinola tribe that had been stealing our babies, we began to find which home each one lived in. It took us months to complete that task. That was when we realized the only children in their village were ours. They had no children of their own. Do you know why?" he asked Uri.

"No." He answered bluntly. It occurred to Uri there were no young people between his sister's age twenty, and his age fourteen. He had never taken the time to look around, and notice such an obvious thing.

Uri sat and listened patiently to Elajon. When his father became quiet, Uri began to speak his point of view.

"If all you say is true and I am truly a Dombara, it wasn't my fault this terrible thing happened. I think it takes more than being flesh and blood to make a family.

"My mother, over there, taught me to walk and talk. She cried with me when I fell and cut my knee. My father, over there, taught me how to hunt, and how to grow up to be a man. I have a sister who fought to save me from those raiders, your people, because she loves me more than her own life. My parents died in a landslide when I was eight, and I don't want another. I am not a little child that can learn to be comfortable anywhere. I'm almost grown. I have my own hopes and desires for my future, and it doesn't include learning to fish or sail a boat."

Elajon walked back to his chair. He sat, leaning forward. "I realize you have had a different life from this one and that you miss your family, your Pinola family. Please understand how we feel, and you do not have to be a fisherman or sail a boat. You have skills and we can learn from you."

Again, Uri was silent.

"Your friend Rill, his parents came and talked to me today. They are having a very hard time with him, and think he should be sent back."

Uri was quick to correct him. "Rill is not my friend."

"Well, you know him and you've been seen together."

"That's true."

"Some older children also want to go back."

"Surely, you must have expected that we would want to go back?" Uri half smiled.

"That is of no consequence. You are all here and will stay here. No one will go back. We will set up more guards at the docks, if we have to."

Uri stood up. "You do what you have to do, and I will do what I have to do."

"Please, try harder Niliab." Elajon pleaded.

"I am going to bed now, good night. We can talk more tomorrow, if you want, but I'm tired."

Elajon stood up and nodded. "All right, good night, son."

Uri crawled into his bed. It was dark in the room, but he could tell Bibbi was awake.

"Were you listening to us?"

"Yes."

Uri knew by the sound of his voice, Bibbi had been crying. "Don't cry. I'm not going anywhere now. I'll tell you before I leave." He lied again.

"Promise?"

Uri rolled his eyes. *Oh, why did he have to say that?*

"You will know when I decide to leave, Bibbi." He hoped that answer would satisfy him. It grew quiet.

As he curled up in the bed, he thought about coming back in a few years and visiting Bibbi. He was the only good thing about this place, and Luwanna of course. His thoughts meandered over to Rill. Those parents got more than they bargained for when they got him back. Well, they won't have to put up with him much longer. Uri hoped Rill would control himself as they started on this dangerous voyage. You never knew about Rill.

Uri yawned and shut his eyes. He fell asleep in minutes.

Chapter Twenty-Six
Saying Goodbye

The next day dragged by. It was the Day of Rest and the parents went to the meeting leaving Uri with nothing to do. He planned to visit Luwanna later in the afternoon, but for now he passed the time by played the Cussel game with Bibbi and Tika.

He noticed looking into Tika's eyes was like looking into his own. That realization shook him. She was shy, but very smart, and had been recently seeing a boy a few years older than her. He was going into the priesthood, and planned to graduate very soon.

"Are you going to see Koori today?' He teased.

She laughed, put her head down, and fiddled with the pebbles. "No, he has gone back to school."

"When will he be finished?"

"Well, very soon. In a few weeks, in fact."

"Then what?" Uri continued.

She blushed, "I don't know."

"Hey Niliab, it's your turn to play." Bibbi said loudly.

"Oh excuse me." Uri shook his head. Sometimes Bibbi irritated him, as a little brother would.

Later in the day, he left for Luwanna's house. Uri began to notice a melancholy mood descend on him. When he returned home, nothing would be the same. No children his age, no Kerka. His relationship with Beka and Suwat could never resume as if nothing had happened. He would have to learn the Pinola's secret, why the abductions? Uri realized he believed the whole story, because the facts were too clear, too obvious. The tattoos on everyone's feet made sense.

He knocked at the door, watching a few children playing close by. The man who opened the door was the same one that had talked to him earlier.

"May I see Luwanna?" Uri asked.

"Come in. She is doing much better. I'm sure all the prayers have made a big difference."

Uri entered and noticed Luwanna sitting on the floor, next to her sister. She was laughing, and smiled broadly when she saw Uri.

"You came to see me."

Her arm was heavily bandaged and in a sling. The bite marks on her face and neck were bruised, but healing.

"I'm glad to see you are out of bed."

"Oh, I feel much better. Here," she patted to the pillow next to her. "Sit."

Uri was uncomfortable with all the family around, gawking at him.

"No, I just came to see how you were. I-I probably won't see you again... for a while."

Her face saddened. "Oh, well I'm happy you're here now."

125

He felt awkward and shuffled his feet. "I have to go." Reaching down he touched her gently on her cheek. "Bye, I'll see you soon. Take care and get better, real quick, Okay?"

She put on a brave smile as Uri started for the door. "Take care of yourself too, Uri. Bye."

He left as fast as he could. His eyes, holding back the tears, burned as he realized there was going to be several people he would deeply miss.

When Uri arrived home from saying good-bye to Luwanna, he laid on his bed fighting the melancholy mood that descended earlier. He didn't come out of the bedroom until long after Bibbi called him to join the family as they assembled in the evening for the worship.

Uri lingered, dwelling on the approaching night. He looked out the window, and watched the Terrasan sunset spread the sky with streaks of red and pinks. He noticed dark clouds rolling in from the north, and began to stretch towards the south. Finally, he joined the family and at dinner, he hardly touched his food, explaining he wasn't feeling well. He saw Bibbi watching as he returned to the bedroom. Later, when his brother came to bed, Uri pretended to be asleep.

Uri dozed fitfully for an hour, his stomach churning. His heart pounding very fast in his chest. He awoke fully and waited as time dragged by. He got up to leave before the appointed time, and went over to Bibbi's bedside, touching his arm. Uri knew that if he was awake he would react, but Bibbi did not move, just breathed heavily as he slept.

Confident Bibbi was asleep, Uri crept out the window, and hunched over, headed for the shadows. He didn't feel safe until the house was out of sight, and he was nearing the docks. In his haste, the wind coming from the east went unnoticed.

Uri slipped over to the hidden boat and looked to see where the shoreline was. It was closer than the night before, and he breathed a sigh of relief. He lifted the back end of the boat and tried to push it toward the water. It was too heavy. He was unable get it started, so he sat down and waited for Rill. It was not long before a figure walked his way. Uri fell on the ground, and lay flat against the side of the boat, hoping it was Rill, not a guard.

"Hey, I see you." Rill walked over laughing. "Scared ya, huh?"

"It's not funny." Uri stood up. "Did you bring water?" he asked, showing his own flask.

"Yah, I did." Rill answered. "Come on. Let's push this boat out to the water."

As they reached the water's edge Uri saw Bibbi running down to them.

"Hey, what's he doing here?" Rill asked sharply.

"Bibbi, go back." Uri cried, alarmed the small boy had been followed.

"I won't tell. When I woke up, and you were gone, I thought I was gonna die. I had to say goodbye." There were tears in Bibbi's eyes.

"Are you sure no one saw you leave?"

"No, everybody's asleep and I crawled out our window."

I'm glad you came." Uri said, relieved.

Rill got in the boat. "Come on!"

"I was very careful. I knew you were planning to leave. I followed you a few days ago."

"And you never said anything to anyone?"

"No. you never told about me when we meet on the dunes, so I never told about you." They both forgot Rill was within hearing distance of their conversation. "I don't want you to leave, but I love you enough to let you go."

Uri was surprised at the wisdom coming from such a young child.

"Please remember what you heard about our Creator." Bibbi pleaded. "It's all true. Everything Father said. Please remember, and remember me too."

"I'll never forget you, my little buddy." Uri affectionately touched Bibbi's shoulder. He felt a lump growing in his throat.

Bibbi was really crying now. "I'll never see you again."

"I'll come back and visit one day. I promise"

"Will you hurry?" Rill pleaded.

"There is something else I want to tell you." Bibbi grabbed Uri hand. "In the old times they spoke a different language. It's called the Ancient Tongue. All our names are from that language, and they all mean something special. My name means Bright Dawn."

"And you are bright, Bibbi. You live up to your name."

"I try to. Your name means something special too."

"What's that?" Uri asked, smiling.

"Niliab means – Great Hunter."

Uri felt a blow between the eyes. No, it couldn't be. He gave himself that title, long ago. He tightened his face, not wanting Bibbi or Rill to notice his reaction.

"Well, whadaya know. I will try to live up to my name too." He smiled weakly. *"Hunter of what*?" He thought to himself.

"Come on Great Hunter," Rill said, his voice dripping with sarcasm. "Hurry up, the wind is getting worse. Let's go."

Uri jumped in the boat. "Goodbye Bibbi. Pray to your Creator for us."

Shocked, Uri didn't know why he added that.

They waved at each other as Rill used the big paddle to push the boat out into the water. Uri hoisted the sail and held on to the rudder, steering them straight to sea. They were off, and the shore grew smaller by the second. He watched until his little brother was only a dot on the horizon.

Chapter Twenty-Seven
Coran

Coran sat in the Great Hall of the Temple. The Temple was the most beautiful building in the land. The Community Building, sitting close behind, came in second. Both were nestled among tall trees, and the meticulously planned landscaping around the buildings meant to be inviting and restful. The silvery blocks that rose elegantly from the land came from an ancient quarry close by, and when the builders finished with the area, they restored everything back to the way it had been. This was the building where Coran came to begin his training, many years ago.

The afternoon light reflected in the narrow windows, creating long strings of colors dancing down the wall, and onto the floor. Coran stared at the rippling colors. It reminded him of the ripples he watched brush the shoreline of the Green Sea fourteen years ago when he was eight years old.

As a child Coran loved to sit at the window of his bedroom, long after the adults were asleep, thinking he was the only one awake to see the stars and moons. That night the weather was balmy, and he watched the familiar twin moons as they proceeded lower in the sky, one after the other, and disappeared behind the distant green hills.

Soon a pervasive darkness covered the land. He listened to the ripples lap the water at the docks, and the gentle wind ruffle the leaves on the nearby trees.

Unexpectedly, there was a movement down at the shore. From his window he watched, first curious, then frozen and terrified as fifteen shadowy figures spread out like a fan, and descended on the village homes that sat at the edge of the Green Sea. The shadows crept, without a sound, between the stone huts, and one by one disappeared inside. It appeared they knew where they were going, and knew what they were there to find. Within seconds, the figures appeared again, and covered by the darkness, made a rapid retreat to the boats lining the shore of the Green Sea that separated two homelands.

Coran sat without uttering a sound, icy fear prevented him from moving or crying out. Within moments of their departure, his young ears heard wailing that permeated every part of the village. Wailing for an irreplaceable loss, for now fifteen families would never be the same. The sorrowful wailing continued through the entire night and on into the following days. Inconsolable, brokenhearted grief permeated space and time, and Coran knew he had done nothing.

Coran forced himself back to the present, and released a great, heavy sigh. He moved his attention from the floor.

The Temple had three areas. In the front was the sanctuary where meetings took place. To the back of the sanctuary housed the priest and trainees, and the dining areas. To the right were the mediation rooms, including the Great Hall.

In the Great Hall, no restrictions existed as they did in the mediation rooms. Here you could talk with others. Coran, at last, felt the need for the company of other worshipers.

His three day, self- inflicted solitude had been broken only when he was called to help with the girl, Luwanna. How surprised he had been at the appearance of Niliab. His cousin seemed to know her very well, and had a strong connection to her. Sadly, that unfortunate incident did much to damage the boy's belief in a loving Creator, and that left another burden on Coran's heart.

To the right sat a friend, Mordan. They both were cross-legged, resting on large pillows. Coran sat for a long time and when he decided to talk, he chose his words carefully.

"Mordan, were you among those sent across the sea to retake the children?"

"No, I wasn't."

"I was." Coran hesitated. "It was very violent."

"I heard." Mordan looked up into Coran's face.

"My spirit is troubled." Coran continued. "Violence is an evil thing. I don't agree with what we did. The older children resisted, and some of the Pinolas were hurt. I myself hurt a girl by pushing her."

"Well, first of all, the deed that caused us to go and take back the children was the first, great evil. Fourteen years ago when the abductions began, our people suffered intense grief. Some parents never recovered."

"I know."

"However good or bad, the Creator uses all things for His purpose. Perhaps beneficial consequences will come from all this. Sometimes His will is not clear to us. We have to trust in Him."

"I have prayed and read the book from the Prophet Hillen, the book on forgiveness and salvation from our Savior. Still, my spirit continues to be troubled."

Mordan got up and moved closer to Coran. "He forgives totally, but you must forgive yourself in order to have peace. I had to forgive also. I had to forgive the abductors, because they took my only child, five years ago."

"I didn't know." Coran touched Mordan's hand.

"She died in those five years. We named her Joi, because she gave us so much happiness. She was three weeks old when they took her. Several men on patrol fought them. They were hurt too. There has been much pain on both sides. However, they began it. Don't blame yourself for anything that might have happened."

"Why...why did they do it? What terrible thing happened that the Pinolas felt the need to do such a thing? Stealing children, how bizarre." Coran shook his head.

"We never found out. You were young when it began, and probably don't remember much. Your family wasn't directly affected."

"No, but I remember, my aunt and uncle's first son was taken. I saw the whole episode from my bedroom window and I never uttered a sound."

"You were only a child."

"I remember after the second time it happened, rumors circulated that the children were being sacrificed to their demon spirits."

Mordan sighed. "Fortunately that wasn't true. We sent spies and they found the children were, for the most part, happy and healthy. That was a great relief. The reason for kidnapping them however, remains a mystery."

Coran felt his body relax, just a little. "Thank you for sharing your memories and thoughts with me." Then he stood, and showing respect, bowed slightly.

As he walked slowly down the long dark corridor that led to his room, he felt very tired. So much to learn, so much to meditate on, and pray about.

When he reached his room, he took his slippers off, placing them next to his boots, lowered himself on the bed, and lay on his back. A great moan escaped him and sad tears began to roll down his face. They fell in his ears and he shuddered. Coran prayed he could find a way to reach Niliab. It would take patience and time.

He rolled over on his side and stared blankly at the reflections through the window. He had gone through much emotional turmoil today. Probably, he would lay awake for hours, but in a short time, sleep overtook him.

Chapter Twenty-Eight
The Green Sea

Uri and Rill hadn't been on the sea very long when the wind began blowing very hard, and it started to rain. Not just droplets, but torrents of water emptied from the sky.

Uri had trouble controlling the sail. Rill had been silent all this time, watching Uri manage everything. He got up and walked to the back where Uri sat, viciously rocking the boat.

"Hey Rill, can you swim?"

"No. Can you?"

"Neither one of us can, so stay down and don't move around!" He had to yell over the howling wind.

They were quiet once again. Then Rill bent toward Uri.

"How come Bibbi talked about the dunes?"

"I have no idea." Uri answered.

"It seems he knew you before we got taken to the Dombara's land."

"What do you mean?" Uri yelled back.

"When he came to get you, when we first got here, I noticed how you looked at each other. Just now he talked about meeting you on the dunes."

"No, Bibbi never said that." Uri hoped Rill would drop the subject.

Again, Rill grew quiet.

The boat was bouncing back and forth in the wild sea. Cold, black waves washed over them as Uri stepped beside Rill to lower the sail.

"What are you doing?" Rill shrieked.

"I have to take the sail down or it'll be shredded by this wind."

Rill got close to Uri's face, and began the accusations again.

"You knew the Dombaras were in our land, didn'tcha? You saw them and met Bibbi when you were on those dunes. Don't lie to me."

Uri became more concerned about the storm and the waves than he was about Rill's wild conclusions. He sat down and held tight onto the sides of the boat

"Sit still, the storm is knocking the boat all over." Uri was losing his grip on the sides.

"It's your fault my mother is dead. It's your fault we were kidnapped because- you didn't tell anyone."

"I honestly didn't know why they were there." He wiped the rain from his eyes.

Rill got nose to nose. "It's all your fault! I should kill you."

"Shut up."

"Don't tell me to shut up. My mother is dead because of you. You..."

"Shut up. Sit down. Why should I care about your mother? My sister could be dead too."

At that instance, Rill jumped on Uri, knocking him to the floor of the boat.

He tried to hold Rill still. "Don't do this. We'll end up in the sea!"

"I'll kill you!" Rill screamed.

Uri felt a blow to his face, and lost his vision for a moment. He wildly hit back. If only he could knock him out, but Uri looked into Rills eyes and saw madness. From those wild eyes, only insanity looked back. Rill leaped again. The boat lurched. Uri looked into the black sky filled with rain. The water rushed in the boat, and over them both. Suddenly they were in the sea.

Waves filled Uri's vision then crashed down on his head. He went under the water and then back up, gasping for air. His hand felt the overturned boat, and clutching for it his fingers found a ledge he could grasp. He hung on and called Rill's name, looking everywhere for a sign of him.

Angry waves covered Uri, over and over again. He tried to hang on to the boat, but his hands were sliding. It was so slippery, so wet. Gusts of wind sent waves over his head, and he fell off the boat into the sea again. He came up kicking, splashing, and trying to keep his head above water. It seemed he gulped in gallons of salty seawater.

Terrified, he couldn't see the boat anymore. He treaded water, it seemed for minutes, but he knew it was only seconds. Then under he went again. When he broke the surface, he couldn't fill his lungs fast enough. He knew the next time he went under he would never taste the sweetness of air again.

Then, his hand touched something wooden. It was that big, fat paddle. Uri grabbed and hung on with all his strength. He bobbed around for a while, barely hanging on as waves continued to leap over him. Then, taking a deep breath, Uri managed to hoist his chest up on it. Again, Uri looked in the sea for any sign of Rill, calling his name only to have it thrown back in his face by the wind. He feared the worst, and put his head down on the fat part of the paddle. The wind pushed the waves over him as he clung on for his life. Tears mingled with the stinging rain, and he began to feel dizzy and disoriented. He had swallowed a lot of salt water just trying to keep above the waves. He began to lose consciousness, and tried to fight the feeling by lifting his head to the sky... then nothing. Blackness won and overcame him.

Chapter Twenty-Nine
The Vision

When Coran opened his eyes darkness covered everything. He sensed it was very early in the morning. The wind was blowing fiercely, and the rain fell like pellets against the window and the outside walls of the room.

He lit the lamp by his bed, and laid back down as the pale light played peek-a-boo on the wall in front of him. He left his parents home to begin his discipleship here and this had been his room. Then two years later the visions began that left him in awe, and in fear, even though he knew the Creator did not give a spirit of fear. Many visions and prophecies later, Coran's reputation grew as a priest that spoke with truth and wisdom.

The vision last night really troubled him. It was more like a dream. He saw many people, hungry and weak. Then, a cage came down from a great cloud, and inside were Ovi's. Their eggs began to drop from the cage. The people caught them and seemed greatly comforted. The same night he dreamed of fishing nets, like the ones his uncle Elajon made. People tossed the nets into the sea, and pulled many fish ashore. Once ashore the nets fell empty at his feet, and the people walked away. What meaning could such strange dreams have? Coran closed his eyes and listening to the storm while he fell into a troubled sleep.

It was just before dawn when he began to dream, or was it a vision? A bright light shone in front of him. So bright, it blinded him. As soon as he was able to see again, he peered into a bright fog and saw a boat in the sea. Somehow, he knew it was the Green Sea and it was near the Great Sand Bars. The storm was throwing the boat around viciously. In the boat was a figure of a boy. He strained to see who the boy was. A large wave washed over the boat, and knocked the boy into the sea. Coran saw him struggling to hang on to a piece of wood. The waves continuously crashed down and the boy reached out to him, a voice, pleading for help, echoed in his head. However, the waves took him away.

Coran bolted upright on his bed. He knew who the boy was and where he was. Coran jumped to his feet, pulled his hair back, and tied it with a leather string. He grabbed for his boots and coat. Putting them on, he rushed out the door, and into the driving rain. He ran directly to Elajon's home, and it didn't take him very long before he was pounding on the door. As Elajon and Marga opened the door, Coran, dripping, fell into the dimly lit room.

"Where is Niliab?" He cried out.

"We don't know. I checked on him when I got up, but he wasn't there." Elajon said. "I went looking for him, but I couldn't find him, anywhere."

'Did you look at the docks, the boats?"

"Yes."

"Oh Coran," cried Marga. "Do you think he ran off with a boat in this weather?" She fell against Elajon. "Oh no, will we lose him again?"

"I had a vision. I saw him in a boat, on the sea." Coran began, but he didn't tell them everything. "I need to take your boat and look for him. He took mine, but I know where he is. Now, this will sound strange. I need to take two female Ovi's and one male with me."

140

"Why?" Elajon was mystified.

"In my dream ... well, the Pinola's need them. If Niliab gets back to his people, they will accept the gift from him. Also, Elajon, I need to give him one of your nets."

"All right, yes, take my boat. The nets are on it"

They went into the back of the house, grabbed three birds, and stuffed them into a cage. Coran ran to the docks. *What if the boy was dead"?* Coran thought to himself. If he found the body, he would take it back to the sister, and give the birds as a present and offering. However, Coran prayed earnestly he would find him alive.

The wind began to die down a bit, but the water still splashed against the boats, bobbed them back and forth. He noticed the sun begin to rise just as he jumped on Elajon's boat. With strong arms, he raised the sail and whipped out to sea. The salt water stung his face, and again prayed he would get to Niliab in time. Coran didn't know if he would find him alive or dead. The vision wasn't complete. They never were.

Chapter Thirty

The Island

When Uri opened his eyes, the sun glared into them with a burning flame. They stung and felt stiff and sore, so he quickly shut them again. He looked between the slits of his eyelids, and raised himself up on one elbow. Stabs of pain radiated throughout his body. His mouth was full of salty sand, and he tried to get rid of it by spitting on the ground. Uri's clouded mind labored to remember what happened, where he had been, and where he was now.

The horror of the storm erupted into his consciousness. Again, he was in those black waves crashing down on him, and he fell back down on the sand, gasping for air. The last thing he could remember was screaming Rill's name into the blinding rain. Sorrow and terror combined, filled his belly, and he vomited salt water into the sand. As he rolled away, he put his face in his hands. Uri knew Rill was gone.

He tried to sit up again. Where was he? He certainly was not dead. There was too much pain. Uri realized he had awoken to a world of sand. Everywhere he looked, north, east, south, and west, sand stretched out in front of him, surrounded of course, by the sea. Somehow, he had washed up on an island, a sandbar to be exact. No trees, no rivers, nothing but sand.

Uri felt the hunger for water erupt in his throat, and he reached for the flask he had tied to his belt. It was still there. He fumbled to untie it and opened the top, but the fluid that

142

reached his lips was contaminated with seawater. Looking at it with disgust, he flung it as far from him as he could. Again, he fell flat on the sand. Without water, he knew he wouldn't last long. He could go without food for days, if he had to, but not without water.

Uri gazed for a long time at the Green Sea, and watched as it lapped at the sand. He had only crossed it twice in his life. Both times were with fear and wretchedness. Now it behaved calmly, and had a quiet beauty he never saw before, not even when he sailed around the Dombara land with Elajon. The glare of the sun reflected off the ripples. No matter how far he looked, he saw only water. He had no idea how far away his land was.

How did he get here? The wooden paddle was all he had to hang on to, and he must have fallen unconscious in the middle of the storm, in the vastness of the sea. He thought he was going to die, but obviously, he didn't. Somehow, he floated here, wherever here was. It was a miracle, but Uri did not believe in miracles.

He bore down on the pain, and slowly stood up on wobbly legs. His sandals were gone, but he still had his pants and shirt on. They were torn and a little stiff from the salt water. He stretched and walked a few steps.

"Well," he said aloud, "at least no broken bones, or bruises." Although his jaw was sore where Rill had hit him.

"*Rill,*" he thought, "*What a fool. We could have been home now, if he hadn't, well… it happened and nothing can change it*".

He walked down to the water where mini-waves hit the shore and wet his feet. Then he continued to follow the water all around the island until he made a complete circle, and was back where he started. It took about twenty minutes to make that trek. He didn't see anything on the island but sand, and nothing out beyond the sea. He had hoped for the sight of land on the horizon.

The sun was very hot and shimmered in a clear relentless, burning sky.

"Well, let's see," he said. "What are my options, or what can I do?"

He laughed, a little hysterically. "I don't have any." and sat down at the water's edge.

"There is nothing but sand. I can't do anything, anything but--- die."

Suddenly Uri was scared and felt alone. He began to tremble. "I don't want to die. I want to go home, just go home." Tears filled his eyes. He began to realize he would never see his sister, Beka or Suwat ever again. He could have stayed in Dombara Land and be alive. Was it a mistake trying to go home? Was it a mistake to think he was clever enough to sail on the Green Sea? Well, the sea won and showed him he needed more than just cleverness.

He staggered back in the direction of the place where he had awoken, and laid on his back. Thirst, again, began to gnaw at him and as the minutes ticked away, his parched lips begin to crack. He knew next his tongue would swell, and stick to the roof of his mouth. Then cramps would tear at his body.

The sun filled the whole sky and enveloped him with waves of feverish torment.

Uri thought if The Creator really existed, and was loving He would help. Elajon said He would be faithful to those who believe and lived for Him. There was nothing else left for him to do. This was Uri's only option.

Again he felt the dizzy, lightheadedness he had experienced in the sea. This time, instead of terror, peace entered his heart and calm light filled his mind.

Uri cried out as load as he could. "Oh Creator of All, if you are real, if you exist help me." His swollen tongue slurring his speech, he sluggishly continued. "Forgive me from all my transgressions and help me die without agony, or save me. If I am worth saving in Your eyes. I will be Your servant and my name, Great Hunter will mean hunter for you. You will be my Savior and I will hunt for all men, so they may know You. I will meditate on Your power and glory. I will learn who You are, and about the Great Savior You sent to redeem us all."

He closed his eyes, knowing he had done what was right and good. A breeze began to ruffle his hair, and the world began to spin in circles. Afraid to open his eyes, he waited, and couldn't tell how much time passed.

Slowly the dizziness diminished, and he felt the desire to sit up. He looked with swollen eyes out to sea. There, far away, he could make out a sail. It was a boat. "No," Uri whispered. "It can't be real. I must be hallucinating."

He watched as it drew near to the island.

"Oh, could it really be true."

He crawled to the water's edge, and stood up. It was Elajon's boat, but it was not Elajon at the sail. Who could it be? He didn't care. He was being rescued.

The boat floated to the shore and a man jumped from the boat into the sea, pulling it along with him in the sand. Uri was incredulous. Could it be? The Creator sent his hated enemy to save him. What was his name, Coran?

A torrent of relief, anger, hate, and joy flooded over him. It was too much for Uri. As Coran approached, Uri's tried to rush him and attack this person who had caused him so much torment. His legs felt like tree trunks, and as he lifted his arms in an attempt to lash out, they hung motionless at his side. Frustrated, Uri knew he was too weak. All the fight left him. His legs gave out and he crumbled to the sand, sobbing, but completely dehydrated, no tears came from his eyes. He was unable to stop. His body shook with the erupting response from deep within his soul.

Uri felt strong arms hold him and a soothing voice in his ear. "Hush, everything is all right now,"

Inside Uri's mind was a glow that expanded from his unconscious to his conscious. The Creator had heard him and sent someone to save him. Why Coran, a man he hated? Uri tried to dredge up that emotion. It comforted him earlier, to have someone to blame for the terrible events, the kidnapping, and the fear of his sister's death, or the very least, injury. Hate would not come. It was gone and Uri realized what a wasted emotion it was. The Creator sent Coran to save him for His purpose. At that moment, Uri felt all the anger and venom seep away into the sand beneath him.

"But I hated you, I wanted to kill you." Uri sobbed out.

"I know. It's Okay. Your sister is fine. I saw her move and open her eyes. I want you to understand, I did not want to participate in that event, but I had no choice." Coran held Uri out from him. "Will you forgive me?"

Uri nodded, "If you forgive me, I'll forgive you."

Chapter Thirty-One
Becoming Cousins

The sky, a familiar blue veil stretched to the horizon, where the contrasting Green Sea filled the remaining panorama. Wherever Uri went under this sky or sea, life would never be the same. Every person he met, old acquaintances or new relationships, he now would view them through the eyes of The Savior.

"Tell me, how did you know I was in trouble?' Uri asked as they sat on the sand. "The Creator sent me a dream that you were drowning. He sent me to save you. Here is some water." He held a flask out to Uri, "Now, drink slowly or you'll be sick."

Uri managed not to gulp the cool water.

"Not too much." Coran warned.

Uri wiped his mouth and handed Coran the flask.

"I'm here to take you home."

"Oh please," Uri pleaded. "I don't want to go back."

"You don't understand. I am taking you back to your Pinola family, back to your home."

Uri tried to control his emotions.

"I'm sure your parents are desperate for you." Coran said.

"My parents are dead. All I have is my sister."

"Oh, I didn't know."

"They were killed in an accident. A fall."

"I'm sorry, Niliab."

"My name is Uri." He replied, sitting up tall, gaining some composure, feeling the water begin to restore his strength.

"Of course, Uri." Coran held up the flask as Uri sipped a little more. They silently looked out to sea.

Coran pointed to the fat paddle Uri had floated on to the island. It rested at the water line. "Well, look at that. Is that what you used to get here?"

"I think so." Uri muttered.

"I made that oar from a piece of wood I found in the forest. I started working on it when I was ten, and it took me three years to get it whittled down. Eventually I was bored and quit. I wanted a big paddle that would fly me through the water, but it ended up to big to use, but I kept it. I worked many hours on it." Coran put his hand on Uri's shoulder. "And it saved your life. The Creator works His wonders in mysterious ways."

"It was right there, under my hand when I needed it." Uri bowed his head. "I'm sorry I sunk your boat."

"Oh well, I hardly ever used it anymore. It was meant to be."

Questions rushed through Uri's mind faster than he could express them.

"You said you had a dream or a vision?" Uri asked. "Does the Savior send you visions often?"

148

"Not very often, but when they come, I must act. I saw you in the water. I knew you were near the islands, but I didn't know if I would find you alive."

"I don't remember landing here." Uri admitted.

Coran chuckled and pointed to the oar that laid by the shore. "You must have floated on it and washed up here. Were you alone?"

The grief of losing Rill to the sea returned. "No. A boy, a – a- friend was with me. His name was Rill. I'm sure he drowned." He resisted explaining the multiple problems Rill wrestled with in life.

"Oh, I am sorry. I am surprised you didn't drown also. It was a terrible storm. The grace of the Savior protected you. It is because of the work He has called you to do."

Uri shook his head, amazed.

"Are you feeling better?" Coran said.

"Yes, thank you, can I have some more water?"

Coran again handed Uri the water flask.

Thinking of Rill's madness, Uri asked. "What happens to people who die without knowing The Savior?"

"Our Savior, the Son came and died a sinner death so we could be reunited with the Father, the Creator. Without accepting Him into your heart, there is no eternity in the dwelling place of The Creator."

"What if a person hadn't the chance to know the Truth?"

"We have to trust Him with that person's soul, just as we trust him with ours."

"There is an evil place, isn't there, with an evil spirit?"

"Yes, the tempter of all creation, the adversary of The Creator."

This was all too much for Uri to understand all at once.

"If I ask The Savior, will He give me visions?"

"I can't answer that. I do know very few people are blessed in that way."

"Then how can I know what The Savior wants from me, how can I show the way to others?"

"You trust Him and He will show you the way." Coran looked at Uri, "Do you believe, and recognize you need to be saved? Do you accept The Creator and Savior as your own Lord and God?"

"My heart is full of Him. It's like I know Him personally, like He is standing right in front of me."

"Then you need to take The Passage of Faith by Water." Coran put his hands on Uri's shoulders.

"Wait, I have had enough of water right now."

"It is commanded by our Lord Savior, to profess faith in Him by passing through water. We can do it here by the edge of the sea. I just pour water over your head as you profess your belief."

"If my Savior commands it, then hurry, do it."

"Uri, I am blessed and honored to."

They walked the few steps to the edge of the Green Sea and there Uri pledged his life to The Creator of the Universe and to His only son, The Savior, and let the Holy Spirit enter his heart.

Uri lifted his arms to the sky, "I can't wait to share this joy with my Pinola family, and everyone back home."

A smile played with the corners of Coran's mouth. "Careful, go slowly. We have tried many times to bring the Good News to the Pinola people. They have rejected and cursed us."

Uri sat down hard on the sand realizing how inadequate he was. "Oh, Coran, how can I do this without any thing to guide me? I'm only fourteen. No one will listen to me."

"You only need to tell people your experiences." A breeze began to blow and Coran looked off in the distance. "We need to take you home while the sea is calm. It can change in moments. We can talk as we sail. Are you ready?"

"Let's go." Uri drank some more, then gave the flask back to Coran and jumped up, staggered a bit. Smiling, he headed to the boat. It was then he saw the Ovi's in a cage. "What are they...did you bring them for me?"

"Another vision. I also brought a net. You will be able to fish for food."

Uri's spirit filled with happiness. He could help his people with these gifts.

Coran hoisted the sail, and they pushed the boat into the water. Instantly the sea took command, and they watched the sand bar disappear.

Uri settled himself in the middle seat on the boat. He lifted his face enjoying the quiet and fresh breeze as it ruffled his hair. He listened to the wind flow through the sail, and the water lap the sides of the boat, while he contemplated new thoughts. He reveled in the knowledge he had been saved to help his people. Not only with food, but also with a message, the Good News of The Savior and of salvation.

"Coran," Uri began, thoughtfully. "I would like to read the Sacred Books, like you have, so I understand about The Creator and The Savior. How can I get those books to read?"

"How well do you read?"

151

"I probably need to go back to school and learn more. When I did go, I really didn't pay much attention."

"Go back to school, and I will try to get a book or two. I could come back in several days and bring one to you. However, I'll have to borrow a boat."

Uri looked at him sheepishly

"If I leave anything for you, it will be in the cave where all of the children were taken. Do you know which one that is?"

"I'll never forget." Uri murmured.

Coran looked up into the sky. "You know, the men who first spread the news of The Savior didn't have any books. They told everyone the marvelous story how He lived, like one of us, and of the miracles they were witness to, and the cruel way He was put to death for everyone's sins to open Heavens doors for all who believe in Him."

"I tell them what I have learned and experienced?"

"There is nothing like a personal experience, a testimony of what The Savior has done for you."

"When you get home, Coran, please be sure to let Elajon, Bibbi and the family know what has happened."

"Surely, it will be a happy time for all of us."

"Someone will need to tell Rill's parents... about what happened. One more request. Will you inquire how Luwanna is and tell her? I think she has become a believer, also."

"I'd be happy to do that."

Uri knew he had a long, hard road ahead, and he set his jaw in determination while he watched the far speck of land grow ever nearer.

Chapter Thirty-Two
Welcome Home

Darkness began it's vigilance over the night, soon after they arrived. They immediately went to the cave. Coran expertly started a small fire to keep away the crawling night creatures. Even with the comforting glow of the fire, Uri felt the clammy air, and it brought back fearful thoughts of that fateful night of the abductions.

He watched Coran put the cages with the Ovis in a corner, away from the mouth of the cave.

"To keep their scent from enticing any animals here." He explained to Uri.

There were three eggs, so he roasted them and soon, sitting cross-legged in front of the fire, they ate a small meal, and fell silent. Now Uri relaxed and put the last two days behind him.

"I wonder how the people will greet me- when I get to the village tomorrow."

"You may be surprised." Coran answered softly.

"What do you mean?"

"I'm sure they will be surprised to see you and you certainly will cause a stir. However, their children are still gone, and they will question you."

"Hmm..." Uri laid back, his arms over his head. "I guess they will."

The stress of the day caught up with Uri and he fell into a deep sleep.

***

Coran left at dawn. They said their goodbyes, and Uri drank some more of Coran's water. It was early in the cool of the morning when Uri made his way up the long, dusty road that led to the Pinola village. Uri was home. Because so much had changed, he was not the same boy that left on that fateful night.

The beige colored dunes rose and fell endlessly along the horizon. The landscape, so familiar to him, now seemed strange and lonely as the bright sky reaching down, sharply contrasted with the dull ground. In his memory, the green of the Dombara land now held a strange beauty, so different from the silent allure of the dunes.

A loud call from a circling bird penetrated Uri's thoughts. It seemed he had been walking for hours. No wonder the Pinolas seldom came down to the sea. It was a great distance, hot and dry. He looked at his feet. The sandals had been lost at sea, so his feet were bare and beginning to get sore. It didn't take long before carrying the cages of squawking birds also became tiresome. Between the sandy road under his bare feet, the heat, and struggling with the cages, he grew increasingly uncomfortable. Well, the quicker he traveled the distance to the village, the quicker he would get some relief.

As he trudged along lost in his thoughts of what Coran had discussed about witnessing to the people, he began to see the edge of the village in the distance.

He would have avoided walking through the village to get home, if it were possible. He couldn't imagine what the people's reaction would be as he returned, and returned alone.

He didn't have to wait long. A cry went up from someone in the village and immediately the people came pouring out, surrounding him. They tugged on him, begged for information about their particular child. He felt as though they were smothering him, and he wasn't even in the village yet.

"Wait, wait!" He cried out. "You are burying me. Please, move back."

The women in the crowd backed off, but some of the men seemed angry and continued badgering him.

"Where have you been?"

"Where are the rest?"

"Are they coming home too?"

"I can't tell you anything unless you all back away from me."

When he felt he could breathe again, he began. "All your children are safe.

They are with their families." There was sudden quiet. "Yes, they were taken to their Dombara birth families, and they are all safe."

"What are those?" A woman asked, pointing to the Ovis.

"They are birds that we can eat, and they lay eggs that we can also eat."

A loud murmur rippled through the crowd. The woman cried out, "We've seen those things before."

"We don't want them." Cried another.

"How did you get back?" A women he recognized as his neighbor, asked.

"Why are you alone?" Another yelled angrily.

155

"I stole a boat and ran away, but I almost died. It is too dangerous to cross the sea."

"What kind of strange clothing are you wearing?"

"We don't dress that way."

Uneasiness tugged at his spirit. What was happening here? Uri understood they felt anger and guilt, but that was no excuse for their rude behavior. Now his anger rose to meet theirs, and he could hear Elajon, *"They are reaping what they sowed."*

They began to harangue him again. What about this child? What happened to that one?

Uri put up both hands. "I can't tell you any more. I don't know anymore. If you want to find out, I suggest you take a trip over there and see for yourselves."

He was done with them and they knew it. Realizing they were not going to get any information from him, each one began to turn in disgust and walk away, leaving Uri without even one person saying how glad he was back, and safe.

Uri noticed the different attitude of the two tribes. He never saw this side of his people before. Now standing alone at the edge of his village where he grew up, and knew most of the people by sight, he realized no one cared. He sighed and looked over to the left of the main road to the village. There stood Beka. Her hair the color of the Brown Hills, her skin, tawny from the sun, and her eyes, the color of bark from the swaying desert trees, now glistened with tears. Uri's heart stopped. He flew to her, and gathered her in his arms. Tears mixed as they hugged.

"Oh, Uri, I thought I would never see you again." Behind her stood Suwat, a wide grin hung on his face.

Uri looked up and saw several people glaring at them. "What is the matter with them?"

'They are jealous, and angry because I have you home again." Beka wiped away her tears, and then she wiped away his.

"Let's go home, quickly." Uri lead them back on the path. "We have a lot to talk about. Oh look, I brought a gift for you." He ran back and swooped up the cage, lifting it for her to see.

"My my, what are those?"

"I'll tell you all about it when we get home." He began to pray in silence. He prayed for patience with these people. It was going to be quite a challenge, bringing them the Good News.

Chapter Thirty-Three
Reunion

The threesome left the village behind, hurrying away from the glaring eyes of the villagers. Soon he walked through the door to the small, mud hut. The familiar sights caused his heart to leap in his chest.

"It's so good to be home." He turned and looked at the two smiling faces. "I didn't know if I would make it. In fact I almost didn't."

He related the storm and the sand bar island, but he didn't mention Rill or Coran by name. As they chatted he realized, they did not ask him any questions about what happened or where the children were taken. He thought that odd, however, they continued to hug and tell him how wonderful it was that he was home.

They fixed an enclosure behind the house for the birds, and Uri showed them how to make nests for them to lay their eggs. Beka didn't seem very sure about it.

"Wait till you taste the eggs. They're very good and healthy too." Uri said.

Then they fixed supper together. After they ate, all became quiet. Uri couldn't contain himself any longer. He looked directly at Beka.

"Why did this tribe, the Pinola tribe, steal all those Dombara children over the years? They told us all about it. Why?"

She laid her hands in her lap and studied her nails. It seemed a long while before she spoke. "I think you should talk to the council, the tribal leaders about that."

"Oh, I will, for sure. But don't you know anything about...why?"

"I was very young, the first time, when you came home as a baby. All I know is that it was done so our tribe would survive."

"Survive what?" Uri grew impatient.

"Please Uri. Wait and ask the leaders all the questions. I am not sure of all the circumstances, and I don't want to give you the wrong information."

Suwat spoke up. "It was all very hush, hush. There were rumors, but one thing was for sure."

"What?" Uri sat forward.

"There were no new babies being born." Uri sat in stunned silence.

"Wait till tomorrow." Beka pleaded. "You can go to the council leaders at the meeting house."

"I guess I have to wait." Uri admitted.

Later, lying on his sleeping mat, the uneasiness he felt in his spirit continued to spread. He realized how much he had changed. He looked at things and people differently. After living with the Dombaras, all he could say is they lived, and treated people with more respect and honesty than the Pinolas. He wanted to live like that.

Uri knew he could never go back to being that aloof, self-centered boy he once was. He knew the Creator of All saved his life and wanted to use him for greater things.

He would not let the elders of the tribe get off easy. They would have to give him a good reason why things happen the way they did. They would have to explain, in detail, their reasoning for kidnapping all those children, year after year.

He fell asleep, but his dreams were of stormy seas and worse of all, he could hear Rill screaming for help.

Uri woke in a full sweat. He sat up on the edge of bed. All was dark except for the kitchen lamp sending a soft glow into the walls. There was a hushed silence in the house. He padded on bare feet into the kitchen to get a ladle of water. Drinking, he heard rustling and whispering in the back yard.

Startled and shaking inside, he moved to the back door. Leaning on it, slowly he opened the door, and peeked into the darkness. Uri saw two figures hovering around the birdcages. Gripping the ladle in his fist, he rushed out the door, yelling and brandishing it like a weapon.

The night air rushed in Uri's lungs and he smelled the clean sweetness. It was dark but the light from the kitchen lamp flooded out onto the ground in front of him. He saw two young men. They looked familiar, but he didn't know them by name. They were always hanging around the village market, not workers or merchants, but bodies taking up space.

The two young men stunned, looked up, tripping over each other as they tried to escape, but Uri reached them before they could scramble away, and blocked their path.

"What are you idiots doing?"

They stopped and stood their ground. 'We only wanted to get a look at those weird birds you brought back with you." The smaller one said.

"Stop lying." Uri replied.

"We heard they were from the Evil Cave Spirits, and they would bring bad times on us." The other spat back. He was taller, older than the first and had an ugly, cruel twist to his mouth.

"Those are just innocent, little birds. You were going to kill them, weren't you?"

"No, no. we're just going to let them loose."

Uri was infuriated. "How dare you, drones of society, to have the presumption to come to my home to do damage. It's not your property." Suddenly, his spirit quickened and he spoke softer. "Do you want to get rid of those evil demons? I will tell you about a Great Creator who has defeated the evil of the Universe."

The two men stood, their mouths opened, gaping in surprise.

"You know what you are doing is very bad, sneaking in here. You have done a wrong to me, to yourselves, and your families. Yes, I heard of a Great Creator who has delivered us all from the evil. Can I tell you about Him? "

The young men backed away. Without a word turned, and ran as fast as they could into the darkness.

"Well, that went real well,' he muttered to himself. Uri felt upset and shaken by this mean, cruel act. He was only trying to help his people. Now, he felt he really botched his first attempt to tell someone about The Creator. What madness did he come home to? He was resolved to tell these people of the Great Savior. He saw how lost they were. Both episodes, the one in the village and now this, illustrated how important this mission was. He sadly wished he could turn back time, and say something that they would understand and contemplate.

Not wanting to go back to bed, he sat in the kitchen and reflected on the night he was whisked away. He thought of everyday in the Dombara land. He thought of the family he ran from, Elajon, Bibbi, even Tika and Suella. How kind they treated him, and how cruelly the Pinolas behaved as he came home. Mostly he thought about the story of the Savior.

Chapter Thirty-Four
Eggs and Explanations

The morning dawned bright and clear. Uri dressed quickly. He continued to wear the long pants he received from the Dombaras, and he longed for the lost sandals. Uri was sitting at the table in the kitchen when Beka came out.

"My, you are up early." She said.

"We had visitors last night." Uri told her.

"What do you mean?"

"I got up to get a drink and I heard noises in the back. So I went out and confronted two young men trying to kill the Ovis."

Beka looked shocked.

"What is the matter with the people?" Uri shook his head. "I've been sitting here all night trying to understand."

"Don't try. They're afraid of new things."

"Even if they are good things, things to benefit them?"

"They don't look at it that way. Just give them time. Soon they will see the benefits." She looked confused. "What are the benefits?"

"Good health and nutritious food. If we let the birds sit on their eggs, they'll hatch, and we will have more Ovis." He continued, excited. "We'll have lots of eggs and lots of birds. Maybe we will be able to trade them at market for--"

Beka cut him off. "One thing at a time. Let's get used to the birds first."

"Fine," He was obviously irritated. "Try an egg this morning."

"Will there be any this soon?"

"They lay every day. We have two females and one male. There should be two eggs this morning."

Together they went and found the eggs. Beka was obviously frightened of the birds. The male Ovi crowed loudly and strutted around the pen.

"They are harmless, Beka. Come closer and see." Uri beckoned to her, and with caution, she walked into the pen.

"They make lots of noise, but they won't hurt you." He reached under the two birds and removed the eggs, then took them in the kitchen.

Suwat walked in yawning, and scratching his head. "Good morning everyone. I see we have breakfast started."

"Good," Uri smiled. "Now we can cook breakfast together."

After they ate the scrambled eggs, Uri ask Beka and Suwat, "Well what do you think?"

"Yes, very good. I feel like I ate meat." Suwat answered.

"Exactly." Uri said.

"I am surprised." Beka admitted. "How do the birds taste?"

"At first I thought they were stringy, but we are used to the wona's meat. It's so soft and tender. I think it's all depends on how the bird is cooked."

"Well, it will be a while before we eat any of them." Beka said.

"The next few days we will let them sit on the eggs they lay. In about ten days, we will have little yellow Ovis running around. However, I think we need to build a better pen. I don't want anything to happen to them."

Suwat got up immediately and began to find tools. Then he went to work on the pen. That left Beka and Uri at the table.

"I'm going to the village this morning alone, and talk to the Leaders."

"I know they are expecting you."

"I hope they treat me with respect."

"You will be fifteen in forty-five days. At that age, you may speak as a man. However, you aren't there yet, so watch what you say."

"I guess they will want to know why I didn't bring all the children back with me. What a foolish idea. It was very dangerous, crossing the sea. I almost drowned, and I didn't tell you, another boy, Rill was with me. He did drown. He was there, with me, and then---he was in the water and gone." He left out Rill's behavior. There was no need for anyone to know.

"How terrible for you." She touched his arm. "I think I know who Rill was. His mother was sick, right?"

"Yes, he told me if he didn't get home, she would die."

"She is dead. She was very ill, and would have died with or without Rill. It would be better if you stayed in Dombara Land than drown trying to get home."

"I had to find out if you were alright. The man who pushed you was very upset that he hurt you."

"Did you meet all of those people?"

"Yes. I lived with my birth family. I have a brother and two sisters."

Beka looked confused.

"Remember, I am not of your blood." Uri spoke softly.

Tears formed in her eyes. "No matter what, you are my brother."

"That is why I came home." Uri laid his hand over hers. "By the way, did you know about the mark on my foot?"

She looked down. "We were told never to talk about it."

"It's a tattoo. It has my name and the family I belong to."

"Mother told us it was an evil mark and never to look at it, or speak of it."

"All the Dombaras tattoo their babies. It has nothing to do with spirits, good or bad. It is only a mark of identification. They looked at our tattoo, and knew what family we belonged to."

"You belong to us too." Beka hugged him tight.

Chapter Thirty-Five
The Secret

Later that morning, Uri found himself standing in front of seven men, the leaders of the village. They sat in small chairs behind a semi-circle of rough wooden tables, and looked as though they had been leaders much too long. Their attitudes matched their stony faces except for two. Younger and hopefully more open to what Uri wanted to say, he looked at them, and allowed a small smile play at the corners of his mouth

"May I sit?" Uri asked boldly.

The man in the middle of the group nodded.

Scanning the room, he didn't see a chair so he sat, cross-legged on the floor

"My name is Uri, my sister is Beka and ..."

"We know who you are, young man." The man seated in the middle spoke.

"Please sir, may I ask who you are then?"

"My name is Pattis, I am elected spokesman."

"Pattis. Thank you for allowing me to meet with you. Since you know who I am, then I assume you know that I escaped from the Dombaras, and why I am here. I want to know why you began to kidnap the Dombara children fourteen years ago. What caused you to take such grievous action? When we arrived in their land they told us the history, from the very beginning."

"It is a long story," Pattis shook his head. "With an unhappy ending." The man was large-boned, and once must have been very strong, but now he slumped over with age.

"Please, I beseech you, I have to know. Why did you cause all the pain and grief?"

Pattis' weathered face expressed a sad aura as he looked left and then right. They nodded in agreement expect for one who glared openly at Uri. A distinguishable red mark on his face quickly identified him as Jai father. Uri wondered if the young men that were after the birds last night were his sons. That family could be trouble.

Unnerved by the new revelations, he had to force his attention back to Pattis and listen as he began speaking.

"Yesterday when word came you had returned we discussed whether or not to tell you the truth. We felt you had a right to know. We have held this secret for so many years, and it is hard to talk about, openly. No other tribe in this land knows the truth."

A shadow of pain crossed Pattis' face and he took a deep breath. "Eighteen years ago a large, burning rock fell from the sky. It landed far to the northwest in the Land of the Sand. We saw it fall, so the young people of our tribe, and their children, set off to find it while the older people stayed behind. Being young and foolish, they treated it as if it was an adventurous lark.

"They walked for two days and found a great hole in the earth where it fell. Curious, many went down into the crater where a large rock had hit the ground. They told us it was very hot. Satisfied, it wasn't something that was sent by the evil spirits to hurt us, they came home." He took another deep breath. "Several days later everyone that had gone down into the crater and a few others began to get sick. They all had the same symptoms. They lost their hair, their skin darkened, and sores appeared. Many died. We had no idea what made them sick or what they died of." He shrugged, "But, life goes on, and so we put the sickness and deaths behind us. We mourned and continued with our lives. However we forbid any of our tribe to travel into the unknown lands of the north, and hung talisman there to keep the Evil Spirits of the North from entering our land as well."

"Did anyone get sick later, after the deaths?" Uri asked.

"No, after the ones that didn't die recovered, there was no more sickness. However, a year went by and we began to notice our women stopped having children. In a couple years, we knew for certain, there would be no babies for our people. The spirits cursed us."

Uri was amazed at what he just heard. "So, are you saying you believed that meant the end of the tribe?"

"Yes, we had to do something. Desperate, we began to plan ways to steal babies from another tribe and raise them as our own. Stealing babies from the tribes close by, of course would not work. We thought if we went across the sea, we could take them from the Dombara tribe. They would never know who it was, and if they found out, we never believed they would come here to take them back. It worked for fourteen years."

Uri looked from face to haggard face. Burnt out old men. Hopeless and defeated. He looked among them for one crack, a fissure in the rock where water, the water of life could seep and spread. None showed any emotion. They gave up so quickly, so hastily with no further investigation. They had not asked for input from the people. Without a whimper, these men had decided they were beaten.

"You accept the death of our tribe as the only solution?" Uri asked them.

"We have faced this outcome for many years." Pattis whispered.

Uri realized there was no desire or idea of how to save the people. "But maybe some new ideas from younger members of the..." immediately he knew, he made a mistake by suggesting this.

The man with the red mark stood, anger radiating from him. "We don't want any of your ignorant advice!"

Pattis raised his hand for quiet. "What has happened has happened. We must accept the curse from the evil spirits." All the men murmured, agreeing.

"What? No wait," Uri stood up. "There is no curse. You are mislead and deceived. I must tell you about what I have learned. The Creator of All has sent His son, The Savior, and defeated the Evil One. There is no curse. There is hope."

The men looked at him with contempt. One, wizened in body and feeble in voice, began to speak. "My son, you are young. We know all about the spirits that live on this land. It is a curse that we have known about and we must accept."

"Are you unwilling to learn about the True Way?" Uri asked.

"There is no other way. There is no solution. We have lost."

Uri stood, attempting to control himself. "Aren't you interested in what has happened to the children? Don't you want to know why they all didn't come back with me?"

Pattis looked up at Uri with surprised and said. "They are safe with their Dombara families. They are gone and will never return. You will be the only one that has come back. The sea is too dangerous. Evil spirits rule the waves."

Uri shook his head. It seemed useless to try to reach these men. Their minds were closed and unyielding.

170

Exasperated he blurted out, "That's nonsense." He paused. "I'm sorry, forgive my impatience. Just listen to me, please."

"This meeting is over." Pattis held up his hand.

The faces closed and shut down. Uri bowed, with respect, but sent a glare to the man with the red mark. He walked from their stoic presence into the open, into a village that had to change, that must change in order to survive. Uri decided, right then, he would go straight to the people. He knew the Leaders did not have the vision he did. The people, his neighbors were the only option left open to him.

Chapter Thirty-Six
A New Way

Uri slowly walked down the path to his home. His mind was whirling, and the people passing to the right and left looked different. Even those he recognized seemed like strangers. Each face appeared stained with grief and hopelessness, their lives having no meaning or purpose. They lived only for their own satisfaction and gain. People lost, without hope. Needing something to bring back a belief in a future.

The task before him was staggering. To bring the knowledge of The Creator of All, His Son's death and resurrection for the sins of the Universe, would be monumental, and Uri felt overwhelmed. At the same time, his heart bled for all of them in their ignorance.

His solitary ways were over. Days of spending time on the dunes were past. He now must go to school, and mix with the children of the other tribes, and learn all he could. Coran said he needed to be able to read the books of the prophets when he delivered them to him. That would be his goal. However, in the meantime he would tell anyone who would listen what had happened to him personally, and make friends with the people of his tribe. A people he had ignored and thought he didn't need.

"The Savior will not abandon these people." Uri said to himself. *"I must pray and listen for His voice."*

172

Coran was right. This is why the Creator saved him, there on that island. He remembered Elajon saying that The Creator used all things to His purpose, and for good.

He was so lost in his thoughts he almost ran headlong into someone standing in front of him on the path.

"Oh," Uri said, startled "I'm sorry I didn't see you." Then he recognized this person as one of the younger council members.

The man smiled, "My name is Denar can we talk?"

"Uh- sure." Uri tried not to sound surprised.

"Will you come with me to my home? I have many questions."

Uri looked into the man's eyes. Looking for that gleam of trickery, or deceit he had grown to recognize in Rill. He saw none, only a pleading soul that seemed to be searching for the truth.

"I'll follow you." He motioned to Denar. They turned down a side path and within moments arrived at a typical home, nothing outstanding or visibly different from all the others in the village.

Denar opened the door and they both entered into a small, dimly light room with a table and three chairs. Several pillows littered the floor and Uri sat down on one.

Denar handed Uri the customary hot drink for invited guests.. Then he sat on an opposite pillow. Uri studied his face. He seemed to be a bit older than Suwat. Wearing his hair short, and his conservative demeanor, is probably what enabled him to sit with the elders.

"I will get to the point." Denar began, "I am interested in what you said about ending the curse, and the evil spirits in this land. Can you tell me what you mean?"

Uri's heart began to race. He prayed a quick prayer, and began. "When I lived with my Dombara family they talked about a Creator of All. I began to ask questions, and learned that a loving supreme being created all of this, the whole Universe, animals, stars, and us.

"At first, I didn't believe any of it. Then I noticed many of the children, the ones taken back, began to accept this belief. When I tried to sail home, there was a storm and I ended up in the sea. I should have drowned, but instead I woke up on a sand bar with no food or water. Slowly, I began to die of thirst.

"As a last resort, I cried out to the Creator, and told Him that if it were His will to save me, I would devote my life to Him. At that moment, I felt a peace descend, His grace and love poured into my being, filling me from my head down to the tips of my toes.

"I looked up, there was a boat coming my way. A priest of this Creator had a vision in the night, and saw me drowning. He even knew where I was. He brought me back to the Pinola land.

"I believe and you can too. I will explain all I know, but I probably won't be able to answer all your questions. I am just beginning to learn."

"When can you tell me more about this?"

"Anytime." Uri replied, hiding his excitement.

"I feel something stirring inside. I want more. I want to talk to some people, so can you return the day after tomorrow?"

"I will come in the afternoon."

"We will be waiting. Thank you. However, you should be warned, you are being watched and must be careful."

"Oh?" Uri hadn't thought about that. "Why watch me?"

"You have been in a strange land and came back, alone. They are suspicious. You begin talking about changes, and a new idea about spirits. The older people are afraid. Be careful, that's all."

Chapter Thirty-Seven
A Measure of Faith

By the time Uri reached home, he was excited and frightened all at once. He went in the house and immediately Suwat brought him out in the back to show him the new pen for the birds. He was obviously proud of what he had accomplished, and was bubbling over with joy.

"See, I have made the Ovi's a house to sleep in at night, with a solid door so they will be safe, and look how high the wire goes."

"Where did you get the wire?" Uri was amazed.

"Oh, I have resources even Beka doesn't know about."

Uri laughed, "Good for you."

"The gate has a lock and if it is tampered with, there's a booby trap." He pointed to a conglomeration of bells and noise making gimmicks.

Uri was impressed. "You are very resourceful, Suwat." He walked back from the enclosure. "Tell me, what do you know about a man with a dark mark on his face? He has a couple of sons that are troublemakers. I think they are the ones who went after the Ovi's last night."

"That would be Zekod. He had three sons, but one named Jai went back, like you. Zekod is not a pleasant character. His

176

sons keep to themselves, but have been known to cause fights in the village a few times."

"When I was with the Dombaras, I noticed how they treated each other. There was such love between them."

Beka had been standing in the doorway. "I never thought about people, other than our family. Except for Suwat. I cared about him. We love each other."

Uri spoke. "Not just our families, but everyone in the whole tribe. The Dombaras take care of each other, share problems, and joys. I never thought of other people either. Now I have a different view on our world."

"Why should we care about families like Zekod's?" She dismissed the whole idea."

"Zekod is someone who needs to know others do care."

She shook her head. "I don't understand what has happened to you."

Uri walked with them into the house, and sat in the front room. "I have discovered a new way, a better way. The spirits we believed in are false. A Great Creator made all we can see, the whole Universe. I know He saved my life to send me back here to bring the goods news of Him and His son."

"That is a strange belief." Beka shook her head.

"No, think about it. Look around at nature, and see the wonderful things He created for us." Uri told them about the fall and the Creator's plan to bring humans back into a relationship with Him once again. They sat mesmerized.

"If those things are true," Beka said. "that's a wonderful thing."

"I will believe." Suwat said. "I always knew there was something good in our world. The superstitions about evil spirits never rang true."

"There is evil in the Universe, but the power of the Spirit overcomes that evil." Uri explained. "I pray to the Creator that He will send the Spirit into your heart and show you the way."

"We need to talk about this again." Beka nodded.

"I am going to meet with some people in a couple days from now. Come with me."

"Yes, we will.' Suwat made the decision for them both. "You have brought back many new ideas. I think they are good ideas, but it will take time for them to catch on."

"We just need to be persistent." Uri encouraged him.

Uri related to them all the Leaders had told him. About the falling rock, the sickness, and about the secret of why, and how the children were stolen and brought to Dombara land.

"I didn't know about most of the story." Beka admitted. "I'm confused, I don't know what to think about all of it."

"Understand... I am here to put an end to the superstitions." Uri declared determined. "And find a way to bring hope."

After dinner of that eventful day, Uri stood in the darkness near the front door of his home. He had just talked Beka into removing the Talisman, and trinkets she placed there a long time ago.

He felt the heat of the day ebbing, and cool breezes begin to ruffle the large, flat, leathery leaves of the Tobanyant tree that grew several feet from his home. The tree grew large, the branches spread wide, angling lower than the top. This allowed the brown, chewy fruit, growing at the tips, easily picked by man or beast.

Uri glanced casually at it, and then something caught his eye. He peered, intently just as a hand reached from behind him, catching him around the neck. Uri began to struggle.

"Just listen Dombara boy. Stop spreading those Dombara lies and ideas. If you don't, you'll be real sorry."

Someone ran towards Uri from behind the tree. It was Zekod. When he reached Uri, he punched him in the stomach. As Uri doubled up in pain, the arm around his throat released, and he fell to the ground.

"Remember what we told ya." The voice from behind him warned.

Uri looked up just in time to see three figures disappear down the path.

Suwat ran from the house, and knelt beside Uri. "What happened? Are you alright?"

"I'm fine" Uri coughed and tried to sit up. "That was Zekod and his boys. They warned me against spreading what they called, the Dombara ways." He groaned. "Help me up Suwat."

As they entered the house, Beka ran over and helped Uri sit down. "We saw something going on," she said, "but it was to dark to see who it was"

"Zekod and his sons." Suwat answered.

Beka looked into Uri's eyes. "Why are they against us?"

"It's not us they're against. They have been bullies all their lives. Zekod taught the boys how to be bullies." Uri shook his head and rubbed the sore area on his stomach. "They picked on their brother Jai. Now that he is gone they have to find someone else, and they will use anything new as an excuse to start trouble. Remember, new ideas will take time. Besides we have a power on our side."

"What did you mean... a power on our side?"

"Do you believe your future can be decided by something greater than yourselves?" Uri asked.

"Yes, I suppose so." Beka nodded.

"The Creator has sent me to bring the Good News and He won't forsake me.

I am persecuted now, but I will prevail. I told you there are some people who are interested in learning more. You said you would go with me."

"Yes, we will." They answered in unison.

Chapter Thirty-Eight
To the Sea

Before the dawn broke, Suwat and Uri followed the road down past the dunes, and into the valley at the foot of the Brown Hills. Suwat gamely trotted along despite his lameness. Uri went slowly, knowing they had plenty of time. He wore the backpack that carried water, food, and implements to start a fire.

"What are nets?" Suwat asked after Uri explained what they were going to do at the edge of the sea.

"Nets are made of... of thin ropes tied together so the fish can't escape."

"Many years ago, when my father was alive, he took me to the seashore and caught fish by hand. He was very good at it, and fast. I used the grag. That worked well."

"With a net we can catch enough to sell at the market, but we'll have to convince the people to taste them so they will buy." Uri stopped and thought. "We could offer samples."

"Oh," Suwat was beginning to understand. "We can use Beka's stand."

"Right."

The sun rose slowly in the east as they came to the rocks and caves of the valley. Uri saw the fear swell in Suwat's eyes.

"There is nothing to be afraid of. I have been in the caves. There are no evil spirits, believe me. Those are just stories." Uri walked inside of the mouth of the very cave he had been taken. "See, come on. I promise there is nothing to be afraid of."

Suwat slowly approached the cave and looked around, his eyes wide with terror.

"This is where the children were taken that night." Uri set the supplies on the ground. "We were so afraid. Not only of the men, but of the evil spirits we had been told lived in these caves." He beckoned, "Come sit next to me."

Suwat limped deeper into the cave, and Uri began to tell him of the events. "We were lined up against the sides of the walls. Thirty-two children, most of them crying for their mothers. It was very sad." Uri lifted his foot, removed the bindings, and showed Suwat the bottom where the tattoo was. "These marks are how the Dombaras knew who we were. All babies are tattooed at birth."

Suwat bent over and examined Uri's foot.

He was speechless and looked back and forth, from Uri's face to his foot.

Uri opened the pack and began to arrange for a fire. "My cousin Coran will be bringing me books and things from the Dombara village. He will leave them in this cave for me."

"Why would he bring you anything?" Suwat asked.

"Because I asked him to bring me a book, and he promised he would." Uri's answer seemed to end the subject.

They examined the net Uri had left in the cave, and took it out to the sea. He taught Suwat to cast into the water off the rocks near the caves. Starting the fire, they cooked the ones they caught, and Suwat admitted he enjoyed the flavor of the roasted fish.

They stood at the bottom of the cliffs as they prepared to journey home, looking out to the sea when Suwat spotted a boat coming ashore.

"Look, Uri, is that someone you know?"

Uri shaded his eyes, and looked out to the shore. "Yes, it must be Coran." He began waving.

Coran beached the boat, lifted something, and headed in their direction.

As he approached, Suwat cowered behind Uri.

"Coran, it's good to see you. I didn't expect you so soon."

They greeted and hugged each other. Suwat watched, his mouth open in amazement.

"Come, meet Suwat, my sister's husband."

Coran grasped Suwat's hand tightly. "It is so good to meet you."

Then he handed a package to Uri. "I brought you a book, and a letter from Bibbi."

That brought a smile to Uri's face. They went to the cave where he took the letter and placed it in his pack.

"Tell me about your arrival in the village?" Coran squatting near the fire.

Uri's smile faded. "Not good. I'm dismayed at the way the people have treated my ideas, and me."

"Have you talked about the Savior yet?"

"Yes and I receive some strong resistance, especially from the older ones, and one particular family."

"Don't be discouraged. When someone asks questions, jump in. Many will be eager for the Good News. His followers experienced persecution and so will you."

"I'm prepared, but I need to pray and read." Uri held up the book. "Thank you my friend."

"I found this book to have the simplest stories of the Creator, and Savior and also about how sin entered the Universe."

"This is just in time. I am meeting with some people tomorrow. Will you stay and join us?" Uri asked.

"Yes I will. I can leave the next morning. I was going to stay overnight here in the cave, but I would rather be with you."

"We are going to take the fish we caught and sell it at the market today. You might be hard to explain." Uri chuckled looking at Coran's clothing, typical Dombara. Also, the flowing robes of his priesthood.

"Would you rather I wait at your home?"

"Absolutely not. This is all part of the new way."

Coran patting Uri on the back. "I'm glad you feel that way."

As they started back up the road to the village, their pouches full of cooked fish, Uri told Coran the secret of the Pinola's tragedy. "The tribe is doomed to perish." Uri's voice revealed the sadness in his heart.

"There must be a solution. You know when the Word begins to take hold, there might be couples interested in coming and minister to the people. They would bring their families, and children would begin to occupy the village once again."

Uri looked up. "I wonder if... some of the older children, in a few years, might want to return to where they grew up and start families."

"I think you are right." Coran nodded.

"They all would bring the Good News with them." Uri's eyes glowed with excitement.

"That means the tribes could unite." Suwat observed.

"I knew there was hope." Uri smiled with satisfaction.

Chapter Thirty Nine
A Change

The noonday marketplace buzzed with activity. Uri had never been in his sister's domain before. Now he would be here often, and not just to sell produce and fish either, but to spread the Word. Even though the Pinola market place was smaller than the Dombara's, all the tribes in this land made their way down here when they needed supplies, produce, clothing, tools, and other commodities.

Fragrances of spices mingled with cooked food wafted over the area, and the fish they had cooked now added to it. A thrumming of background conversations permeated the whole area. As Uri walked around with Suwat and Coran, he enjoyed meeting the people. "Here," he offered. "Try this. It's fish from the Green Sea. It is fully cooked, try it." persuading more than a few into trying a bite of the morsels. They all looked suspiciously at Coran, but no one said anything.

They ended up at Beka's stand and Uri introduced Coran to her, with caution, not wanting her or Suwat to know he was the abductor that night.

Many people were curious about the fish, and crowed around Beka's vegetable stand. Just as Uri finished discussing the art of catching fish with a friendly man, he looked up into three scowling faces. Zekod and his sons, Pishob and Turik.

"Would you like to try some?" Uri boldly offered a large hunk of fish to them. Zekod glared at Coran. "We don't want any of your Dombara food or your Dombara ways."

"What's wrong with being a Dombara?" Uri asked. "Jai is one."

"Yea, we always knew there was somethin' wrong with him." They laughed coarsely.

"You might like to know Jai is very happy." He couldn't refrain from adding, "His family is well off and very important in the village."

"Who cares about him?" The taller one, Pishob remarked and spit into the ground.

"Well, he's better off." Uri finished. "And don't worry, he won't be back."

"What about Rill?" the other asked.

Uri's head shot up and his stomach leapt. "What about Rill?"

"Well, is he better off? Will he try and come back?"

Uri glared at them, one at a time. "I don't know if Rill is better off, but I do know he won't be back."

"Huh, that's too bad." They snickered. "He's missed." They lifted their heads, laughing and began to move along. "We're keepin' our eye on you, Dombara boy." They shot back at him.

Uri wondered if they asked about Rill because they enjoyed picking on him, or if he was a cohort in their mischief.

"Are those the bullies?" Coran asked.

"Yes." Uri nodded, and watched as the three turned the corner and disappeared.

Late in the afternoon Beka packed up the vegetables she didn't sell, and they all left for home. They saved some fish, and with the vegetables, they made a scrumptious meal that night.

The night air was cool as they sat outside by the door enjoying the breezes, and the sounds of the birds as they flew back and forth in the trees, singing their evening songs.

Coran was first to speak, "Beka, have you noticed a change in Uri, since he's been back."

"Yes, I have. He used to be very quiet, and enjoyed being alone a lot. Now he seems to have a new purpose in life. He talks to everyone, and even wants to go back to school."

"I think he is happier, and he has a peace about him I never saw before." Suwat said.

"Good changes, right?" Coran asked.

Beka reached over and held Uri's hand. "Yes, something has changed."

"What do you think it could be?"

"I think it's his new found faith in The Great Creator." Suwat smiled.

Uri sat forward, he closed his eyes, and a smile grew wider.

"Yes, I have found the meaning of my life, and the meaning of all life. Beka, do you understand what giving your life to the Savior means?"

"No, I am confused. We only believed in the spirits we were told live in this land."

"That was a lie." Suwat answered. "The elders kept us blind with those superstitions. I believe Uri, I understand."

188

Coran stood up and stretched, "Tomorrow we will go to the meeting, and Beka, maybe your questions will be answered. Now, I will say goodnight."

They took their time retreating into the house and retired for the night. Uri made a final check on the Ovis, then lay down next to Coran.

"Thanks for not mentioning the night you took me away. She doesn't know it was you."

"Obviously God orchestrated all of it, and He has a greater plan to fulfill."

Uri stared into the darkness. *"Obviously He does"*. He said to himself, and shut his eyes.

Chapter Forty
An Accusation

In the early morning, Uri immediately went out into the back and gathered the eggs from the Ovi's nests. It had been a couple of days so there were several eggs left for him to fix for breakfast. He left three behind, under one of the hens.

The conversation was casual. Everyone began to enjoy breakfast, when a knock came from the front door.

Beka went to answer, and then looked back at Uri. He motioned for her to go on. She opened and peered outside. Two men bowed slightly.

"If you please, the boy Uri is requested to appear at the Meeting House as soon as possible. The leaders of the Elders are waiting. We will escort him."

Uri walked to the doorway. "Am I being arrested? I have broken no laws."

"No, you are needed to answer some questions."

He put on the sandals Coran had brought him and turned to everyone at the table.

"I'll be back soon."

"Wait," Coran called out. 'I'll go with you."

Together they followed the men into the village and to the meetinghouse.

Once again, Uri stood in front of the elders, this time with Coran next to him. There were only three of the elders present.

Pattis motioned for them to sit. "Thank you for coming on such short notice."

He looked at Coran. "Who is this?"

"He is my cousin Coran." Uri began. "He is my guest here visiting me."

"He is a Dombara." One to the left of Pattis stated.

Coran bowed with respect. "Yes sir, I am a Dombara, and a priest of my faith."

Uri stepped forward. "Am I not allowed to have someone here, with me?"

"He may stay, however he is not to speak." Pattis said.

"I shall hold my tongue." Coran nodded.

"Uri, there has been a complaint brought against you. It seems you have been causing a commotion at the market place, and are keeping dangerous animals in your home."

"Who has brought this complaint? I have a right to know and confront my accuser."

"This is not an inquisition, we only are asking questions. Do you admit to these complaints?"

"No, what proof do you have?"

"Zekod has told us of a problem at the market place yesterday."

"He threatened me, and the night before he and his sons attacked me in front of my own house. Zekod is a grown man and he punched me, a boy, in the stomach. If anyone has a right to complain, I do."

"Are there any witnesses to this attack?"

"Yes."

The three men murmured together.

"We want to ask you one more question. Are those birds behind your house dangerous?"

"Absolutely not. They are for food. They are not more than 12 inches high and eat vegetables."

Pattis sighed. "Finally we want to sternly warn you about spreading lies about the Spirits that dwell in this land."

"I do not lie about the spirits. However, I will not stop telling the truth about the Great Creator Spirit. I have broken no laws. On the other hand, go back to Zekod and question him and his sons about trying to kill those birds, threatening me, punching me, and grabbing my throat. There are laws against destroying other people's property and doing physical harm to another."

"We will check into those accusations. You are dismissed."

Coran and Uri stepped out into the heat of the day and looked around at the village activity. Uri shook his head and gestured back inside where the three elders had questioned him.

"They are such fools, such blind fools." He kept repeating.

"The Creator is using you to teach them something. Be patient and allow His will to be done."

***

192

The afternoon began hot and windy. The group trudging along to the home of Denar included Uri, Coran, Suwat, and Beka. As they entered, all four were shocked. A dozen or more people sat, waiting for Uri to arrive.

Uri leaned into Coran. "I'm sure glad you're here."

Denar come forward, "Welcome, we have a place for all of you to sit." He motioned to an area in front of the group.

Uri took a deep breath, looked sideways at Coran, and began to introduce him to the people gathered.

"Coran is a priest of our faith. He is my cousin and my guest. He graciously agreed to join us today."

Coran stood and bowed slightly. "If you are here I assume you are interested in knowing about The Creator of All and His son The Savior. I will tell you the story of creation and how the Universe fell into sin and chaos."

He went on to explain the fall of creation and the Creator's son, sent to save the Universe, and by sacrificing His life He defeated evil. Coran explained that each person has evil in him, but because of His great love, the Creator will forgive every sin.

The people seated around gave Coran their complete attention. Every eye fixed on him with his Dombara clothing and the purple priest's robe.

"By dying He restored mankind throughout His creation to Himself again. Whoever believes in Him will be with Him after death eternally. The greatest evil spirit cannot destroy that relationship. When the people believe and accept The Son's death for all sin, love will prevail. The superstitions will disappear. It is only a superstition that this land has evil spirits roaming around.

"There are no evil spirits in the caves. I know I have been in them." Uri added.

193

"Fear and superstition, yes I can understand that." Denar nodded. "Please continue."

Two hours later Uri and Coran still were answering questions from the group. Uri, delighted with so much enthusiasm from everyone, hadn't notice Beka's tears streaming down her face. Finally when Coran called for those who wanted to ask the Lord and Savior into their hearts, Beka was the first to stand up. At last, Uri's whole family was under the Creator's love.

Eight souls came to the faith that afternoon. It was more than Uri expected and his heart felt as though it would burst. Uri was delighted when he saw one of the older men of the council and his wife among the new believers.

"This is a miraculous start, Uri." Coran said as they began the trek home.

Uri walked beside Beka, his left arm around her and his right around Suwat.

"I am amazed. The people seemed to long for something that could bring them hope."

"They even were interested in the Ovis." Suwat said, and then added proudly. "I invited them to inspect my cage."

"Well, we will need to start letting the birds hatch some of their eggs." Uri said.

"The next time I come visit, I will bring a few more. Maybe some chicks too." Coran offered. "If you don't mind, I would like to stay until morning and leave early."

"You are welcome to stay as long as you want, and come back anytime." Beka said. "You are family now."

Chapter Forty-One
Hope for the Future

The setting sun poured out it's gold on the sand dunes, causing a gleaming sparkle in the dusk. Uri and his family settled in for a restful evening of conversation about the day and made plans for further meetings in the village. Uri related the complaints of Zekod, and all that transpired with the council.

"I don't think we have to worry about them again." Uri sighed.

"Don't let your guard down." Coran warned. Then together they prayed for Zekod and his family, they prayed for all the families at the meeting that day, and they prayed for each other.

After saying goodnight, Uri relaxed as he sat on his sleeping mat. The day had been exhausting and wonderful. He never felt so weary and excited all together before.

Uri touched the book, eager to read the stories its contents would reveal. He fondled the letter, savoring the thoughts of what was inside. Slowly he opened the flap of the envelope, took out the single page, and spread it on his lap.

Uri's reading ability needed improvement, but school started tomorrow and he would be there, and everyday thereafter. Knowing he would be the only boy from the Pinola

195

tribe caused some apprehension, but there were a few Yoka boys he remembered from last year. It might not be so bad. Besides, he would get the opportunity to share the Good News with them.

Coran would leave in the morning for Dombara Land, and he would be alone to instill the Good News into the hearts of these people. Today was a good start, however he knew he had to minister to the new converts. He was a new convert too, but The Creator had placed a special mantle on him. Plans had to be set to have regular meetings. Denar offered his home for those meetings, but Uri wondered if that would jeopardize his seat among the elders. Well, Denar would have to deal with that.

He placed the book on the bed lovingly. This book would answer many questions people would have. In addition, many doubts would be raised, and it would help him to be ready.

He picked up the letter and began to read what Bibbi had written, stumbling over quite a few words.

"Dearest Uri, Coran told us about the rescue, and of your miracle. We were so overjoyed at your acceptance of The Creator. Our parents cried for hours. Not only because you didn't die in the sea, but knowing the Creator chose you to be His messenger.

More good news, Tika is to be married to Koori. He finished his training as a priest and they decided to be joined right away. In five days we plan a big celebration. He has lots of family. After prayer and much discussion, they plan to come and minister to the Pinolas. Can you believe that? When Koori heard your story he announced that was his mission, and Tika agreed. Shy Tika. I can hardly believe it. I wish I could come too.

I miss you so much. I pray things will be easy for you and that you are enjoying your Pinola family. Maybe some day we will all be one.

Love, your brother forever, Bibbi

Uri laid the letter back in his lap, and gazed out the window. He wiped the tears from his face and sighed. When would he see his little brother again? Uri wondered about Luwanna, and if she was recovering from the bites of the Getiru. Maybe she would write him as Bibbi had.

The moons lit the desert sky with a glowing promise of a bright tomorrow, one that would contain both joy and tribulation. A glorious tomorrow held in the hands of the Creator.

Epilouge
A Conspiracy That Leads to The Dengue Odyssey

Even as Uri and his family prayed for Zekod, evil forces gathered around a far removed dwelling. It was more of a hut than most of the homes in the village. It sat alone at the outskirts of the village, surrounded by dirty pens where a few animals scattered about, living in their own filth. The residents lived no better than the animals they kept.

The contents of the home displayed disruptive chaos in which the degenerate occupants existed.

It was dark in the home. No light could survive any length of time, because the pervasive evil was great.

Nevertheless, a dim glow came from under a door at the back of the room. That was where the women stayed until the men were finished with their business. The glow wasn't enough to allow them to accomplish any task. However, it held them captive in its allure.

The odor throughout the hut was a combination of sour food and musty clothing. The stale and heavy air resided comfortably with the darkness.

Zekod, his sons, and three other men kept their voices low. This was their first clandestine meeting, but it wouldn't be their last.

Zekod was talking. "We mustn't loose our grip on the village. Today the council questioned him about the accusations I brought against him. I instilled the thought that the fear of the spirits must continue intact. I can handle the Elders. You have to circulate among the people. Listen to the gossip. If the villagers begin to talk about this Creator we have to put an end to it right away."

"They may not listen to us." One of them spoke up. "I heard a couple of the council members are sympathetic with their beliefs."

"I have another plan, but it involves our friends from across the sea, the Bast. I don't like dealing with them unless I have to. However, they have some interesting methods. Using those methods, we will cause more fear, and our power over the people will greatly increase."

"What methods are you talking about?" the older son, Pishob whispered.

Zekod leaned back in his chair. "We can discuss that if it becomes necessary.

Right now we must bide our time. Let's take it slow, keep it simple and among us."